Title: Three Very Different Women
Author: Stuart Bonnington
ISBN 978-0-9944362-7-6

© 2022 Stuart Bonnington

Editing and production by PB Publishing, Gisborne Victoria
Printed by IngramSpark Australia
Dandenong Victoria

ACKNOWLEDGEMENT: The use of poetry from many sources that I enjoy so much.

Dedication

To Jay, for the huge help given and full
encouragement to keep at it.

"No matter how bad the prose is,
it might be verse"

Contents

1
Linda Alexander

Linda Alexander is a successful career police officer based at Melbourne Central head office in Victoria, Australia. She has worked her way up through the ranks from her early start in the academy in Perth, Western Australia, where she was selected straight from university, not long after she and her family had arrived from Johannesburg, South Africa. She had easily passed the aptitude and attitude requirements plus medical health and fitness tests to enter the police force.

Linda was appointed to Claremont station in Perth, where she was greeted by a mixed reception — ranging from respect as an exemplar of the new modern-style regime, to the old 'women can't do the job' — and to a genuine welcome from the senior sergeant there. She was given no special concessions and was included in the tough and boring assignments like stake-outs. She naively fell into a sexual relationship with an older married officer who unceremoniously dumped her when the relationship was questioned. The disappointment and humiliation felt by the twenty-year-old motivated her to apply for a transfer to Victoria. This was successful and Linda timed the move with a quick trip back to South Africa to visit her ailing Granny. The words of wisdom from her grandmother, mixed in with the sympathy for a broken heart, were "to enjoy the job, seek higher educational opportunities, and embrace all the benefits of being an 'Aussie'." The family had been able to enjoy the privileges of the past in South Africa, but apartheid was totally unacceptable to them.

In Victoria, Linda was fortunate to be posted to Footscray Police Station where she was warmly welcomed and given opportunities to be involved in detective cases, which was her chosen path. The first case of significance was what became known as the Ballarat Shop Bomb, or the 'Melting Pot Murder' case. This involved an antiques shop in central Ballarat managed by a mysterious, reclusive ex-Royal Australian Army Service Corps soldier, and previously owned by an elderly woman who had willed the property to her nephew, a Ballarat university student called Glen Robertson. Products sold at the antique shop had included drugs. The investigations included possible connections in New Zealand. Linda was complimented on her work in the case, made new associations and moved up the ranks within the police force.

Sometime after the successful result and with her higher rank, she was allocated to assist in a second case, dubbed the Macedon Ranges 'Double Jeopardy' case. This was a disturbing case involving the brutal murder of the twin Moretti brothers over unpaid debts for illegal tobacco, alcohol and drug deals. Superintendent Ron Brunton had specifically invited Linda onto the case that was based at the Gisborne Police Station. The case was particularly gruelling as it involved extreme violence including the amputation of fingers of both twins. Investigations included connections in Adelaide and Sydney and the need for search warrants interstate. For the first time Linda was exposed to international crime syndicates and their vast power.

Linda often thought of her old Granny's favourite saying, "The world is full of strange and weird people except for you and me, and even you can be strange!"

Now based in the Melbourne Central headquarters with her own small specialist team that was allocated special 'projects', Linda — now a Detective Inspector — was recognised as having high-level promotional potential.

Her private life was indeed very 'private' and she lived, as would be expected, a super-clean regime. She shared accommodation with her brother Brendan (a senior corporate executive) and had a comfortable long-term partner, Jeremy, with no current plans of marriage or children. Linda had a close female friend and associate in the police named Beth Jenkins, with whom she had previously worked in two cases. Beth had now been promoted to Sergeant based at Woodend Station so, when possible, the two got together over coffee to catch up. Almost like therapy for them both.

Now in her early thirties, Linda was a fitness fanatic and enjoyed playing in team and single sport competitions when available. She enjoyed gym work and was fit and trim. Her work appearance was always very professional with her hair tied back and conservative clothes indicating her position and rank. Private clothes were different! Her neat and trim figure allowed her to wear tighter-fitting colourful clothes and to add extra colour with silk scarves, colourfully framed glasses and more colourful, slightly higher-heeled shoes. And the occasional ribbon to loosely hold back her long flowing hair. She was really attractive.

She was still a voracious reader and enjoyed learning, and gaining further education was a priority.

Within the police force, DI Linda Alexander now reported directly to Superintendent Ron Brunton, and had reporting to her as a Deputy Inspector, Ian McDonald. Both relationships were strong, vigorous and respectful.

The investigation currently being worked on was the strange case of Gus, aka 'Gussie' Graham. The Piano Man.

During the years of Linda's growing maturity and climb through the ranks, her gaining of ever-more educational qualifications both inside and outside the police force, her increasing expertise and experience, there was another young woman growing her life in a parallel but very different way.

Her name was Helen Murphy.

2
Helen Murphy

Helen was thirty-plus, experienced in life, and now a well-educated young woman, but as hard as nails. She also evinced a strong narcissistic personality disorder.

Helen's childhood and everything associated with it was memorable only for its unpleasantness; she had no recollection of her father, and a toxic relationship with her two older siblings, Gordon and Daphne. Another older sister had died at birth. Her mother, a single mum existing on welfare and community handouts, was a downtrodden wreck in constant fear of her current (usually a monster) partner. Everyone in or associated with the family had huge hang-ups about how they should be treated. There was immense resentment for being what they were, i.e. dirt poor and uneducated.

Helen progressed through life with an inbuilt protection of numbness. When inevitable attitudes surfaced that took her by surprise, she did not always recognise where they had come from. She certainly never knew her father, or even who her father was. Her mother had been under eighteen years of age when she began having children and had then made every effort to deposit Helen in some form of foster care. The quality of that care varied almost as much as the weather and involved the luck of the draw more often than not. The odd caring family smothered her in affection, but when that stay came to its conclusion it left Helen aware of the good care and love that could exist, which then made the bad and ugly life experiences even more bitter.

In Helen's childhood, the surname Murphy added an identification of Irish extraction which sometimes had consequences. In all, an absent father, an immoral, sloppy and talentless mother, and vengeful older siblings made her childhood years very ugly. The Australian foster care authorities tried to minimise the hurtfulness of just surviving by encouraging her on the road to academic success.

Helen was small in stature, with slightly ginger hair and freckles, and was bullied and humiliated by other pupils and even teachers on occasion. She could be feisty under pressure, and when in frustration and anger she did strike out physically and violently, that only added to her punishment. On at least one occasion a male teacher took liberties with her small body and attempted sexual activity. Unreported of course.

At a very early age Helen learned to hate and she planned her exit from her enforced miserable circumstances — and revenge — even though she had not refined the methods that would make her exceptional one day. It did not take her long to learn how to lie and cheat, and how to make use of activities that were out of the norm. She became bold, audacious, with no loyalty to anyone or anything, as each insult or harm inflicted on her heightened the hate and revenge burnt into her psyche, to be used later for repayment. She learned to control her burning anger and resentment within, stored for later use. A very mature, if alarming, attitude in one so young.

Helen understood this was such a game-changing attitude that she would hide her intention behind a wall so she could not be judged. This would need a subtle long-term plan and draw on her understanding of 'normal' type behaviour.

Helen Murphy was definitely twisted, evasive, full of angst, but not in denial, and was mainly able to cover most of the warning signs with her high intelligence. She could lie with such charm because she had an exceptional memory. She had had generous treatment from some foster parents. Probably her most pleasant experience was with a family who had their own daughter of similar age to Helen, who generously welcomed her as part of the family, which included a much-loved Cocker Spaniel. When it came time for Helen to leave, she made unreasonable and unpleasant demands to take what she now considered to be 'her dog' from her new sister.

Life can be unfair, and lessons can be hard to understand when so immature. As a child, Helen could clearly recall the silly games and attitudes imposed on her by female carers who always seemed to insist on babyish things like treasure hunts and easy solutions to puzzles at the same time as insisting on no aggression in play, and always making her the silly little girl in frocks. Females were considered inferior and most men took advantage. So be a good girl and behave!

3

Helen: Early Life

Helen Murphy had been a small and physically undeveloped child, but with such a surprisingly winning smile that many teachers and social workers made efforts to include and involve her in opportunities and activities for advancement. She quickly identified chances to reinvent herself and give herself opportunities to grow her burning ambition to succeed, and to also be recognised and acknowledged.

One of her former friends said, "You always win — how come?"

Helen's reply was, "I work really hard at everything I do!"

She was very secretive about her family and the foster care she had endured. Personal history was a no-go area. Helen knew she could attract attention from boys and men and — probably deep down learned from her mother — she believed that women had it tough simply because they were women.

Secondary school was an adventure in growing up. Because of some family bad behaviour, Helen was moved by childcare and social welfare supervisors to a new school in an older suburb, where she was welcomed into a tough group who blatantly bucked the rules and behavioural expectations, and openly bragged about smoking cigarettes and using marijuana. That did not last long, as social workers, vocational advisers and police intervened and tried hard to give guidance. Life progressed quietly for several months until Helen — somewhat amazed — realised she was pregnant. Yes, she knew full well how that happened because in her own sly way she had enjoyed the warmth of the bodily contact necessary, even though there had been no discussion about the word 'consent'.

To Helen, the father was just a boy of no consequence. One of her girlfriends asked her if she needed an introduction to someone to talk about her options. She asked Helen if she was sure of the pregnancy and if so, how long gone.

The confident reply was, "Eight weeks."

Being so sure because of her own research, Helen was able to enlighten her friend. "You know that at this stage of a pregnancy there is little more than a scrap of small cells not much bigger than a thumbnail," she said. "The point is that I have absolutely no emotional connection to it even though I know the father, and I'm not going to tell him."

It was obvious that Helen would not be consulting her own mother, who clearly had never been an ideal parent, so the quandary was simply from whom she could get guidance to terminate the pregnancy. Discreet enquiries lasted little or no time before a social welfare department employee was on the job. Questions galore in every direction. Were there any signs of Helen being a heroin user? How would a fifteen-year-old survive and thrive with no apparent income? Was she struggling to let go of her childhood history? Who would authorities be most interested in protecting the welfare of: mother or new child? Should the police be involved about under-age sex and protection for the future?

First things first — a GP would be needed to confirm the pregnancy and give advice. A cynical bureaucrat, newly appointed, theorised to all and sundry that such a visit would take approximately fifteen minutes: the opinion from the doctor about five minutes and the rest of the time in form filling. It sounded formidable for everyone concerned but the outcome was that the GP recommended that because of the 'Hollywood worthy' drama put on by Helen, it would be best all round to terminate the pregnancy forthwith and have Helen sent off for further assessment within Social Services.

4

Reinvention

After many months of assessments, and many medical and psychological tests by Social Services, it was finally decreed that Helen Murphy was highly intelligent, if somewhat manipulative. She was deemed to be serious in manner, lacking in natural humour, with no obvious physical abnormalities, nor violent tendencies.

Helen by now had decided that she wished to become a teacher. With support and the consensus of the experts it was agreed to recommend she be given approval to apply for entry into a college that would allow a pathway to an education degree. This was managed and she was admitted as a pupil in February of the new year.

Helen could not have been happier. She was inside still a 'wannabe' with deep hidden feelings of an emptiness, but she was determined to reinvent and re-establish herself as someone of a special category. She took advantage of the short holiday before she was expected to commence her studies by beginning a physical training regime aimed at refining her natural sporting talents into a new physical hardness that would give her greater endurance. She also trained up on personal protection routines that could adequately protect her from any physical attacks.

5
Becoming a Teacher

Helen settled down and spent the year studying at the college, undertaking part-time work at the same time, and then gaining an admission to a university to undertake an education degree. She was not yet fully aware of a developing attitude within herself that it was all males who were her main rivals and antagonists, but in her mind, she had already clearly categorised most men into one of three categories, and she recognised them all at university:

– the eager 'Ivy Leaguer': Hell bent on qualifications and don't get in my way!

– the slick 'Wall Street Hustler': Great fun and knew the value of money.

– the sensitive 'Smart Boy': Would make a great teacher and be a good friend.

Of course, there were some other types. Cool-arse types, feral love-jackals, noisy acrobats, and the porn 'stars' — all in their own minds. Helen and her friends referred to them as 'Pathetic Peckers'. Her new-look physique most certainly aided and abetted her progress in her career path particularly by men who thought they were the bees' knees.

Helen was subconsciously heading down the slippery slope to implementing a secret and ugly attitude, unspoken and as yet not admitted to anyone. 'Aggressive rivalry — because you are male. Make all men's lives unhappy! Society is unfair to women!'

In her new and very determined public persona and with a deep ambition to achieve, Helen ruthlessly planned to use friends and acquaintances as stepping stones to advance along her life's journey. Part of her overall plan was to make herself physically — and even personality-wise — as attractive as possible. Now a very taut and slim figure, with slightly bowed, shapely well-tanned legs and square shoulders, her smooth skin and large dark brown eyes completed her look. Sparkling white teeth were noticeable when she chose to smile.

Helen's biggest challenge was to hide her inner feelings. She was not popular because she was often hurtful with her personal criticism of close acquaintances, and occasionally was downright rude to them, as she had yet to acquire the social skills she needed. She was very good at sport and particularly at hockey, where she could be aggressive and get away with the odd really nasty shot. Her unfortunate childhood had deprived her of exposure to the more genteel sports and activities that could be helpful in social progress e.g. tennis, golf, bridge etc.

Helen passed all the necessary exams with ease and her sharp intelligence was noted by her university tutors. She was quick to realise that success was a useful cover for shortcomings — of all types — and also a cover if some aspects of what was considered 'normal' in a person were missing.

She had many derogatory terms that she applied internally to people and two in particular kept rising to the top of her internal resentment list: the 'Super Mum' and the 'Man Hater'. This was not a good attitude when training to work with other young men and women to become educators of young people.

The 'Super Mums' were easy to identify and easy to feel zero connection with, because Helen had decided that she did not want to have children of her own. She was scathing in her own mind about those young mums whose entire world revolved around their (always) superior children; children who were so admired by them and whose attributes were pointed out to every lesser soul in the universe. The 'Super Mums' were always pointing out to the other young mothers lucky enough to be in the same small bubble the mistakes other mums were imposing on their 'lesser' kids in the same privileged atmosphere. How wrong and damaging that was to them. Will the children ever be grateful? Don't those with women sons create a dilemma by favouring the boy throughout his life? And having children wrecked your figure for ever! And what about the mother's own personal development? Helen's list was endless.

The Alpha Male most certainly existed everywhere in Helen's mind. 'No wonder women became Man Haters' was her thinking. She was certain it was all about cultural attitudes, and with history to blame. Even now, there were only two streams to growing up; separately male or female. She knew for a fact that male violence to women and particularly to those super mums with kids, was disproportionately high. She internalised it very deeply.

Helen's plan was to use her own internal resources and in particular, with great caution but with much confidence, her own body. She had recognised that the discreet use of alcohol was an aid. Without any family or close personal attachments, she had no distractions to interfere with her grand scheme. She could utilise herself to the height of selfishness and self-focus. Her years exposed to bureaucratic and professional guidance and her negative social interactions had prepared her to be able to plan, and know and use her body to achieve results in many ways.

Helen — through other people and her own explorations — began experimenting in creating extremes of sensual pleasure. In the past, the necessity for care and cleanliness had been stressed to her by the medical profession, and she observed this emphatically, having been made aware of various sexually transmitted diseases. She was well aware that with her trim breasts some emphasis on them could be valuable. Her areolae and nipples were naturally dark in colour, and she was not averse to soft massage around her breasts. She had all the weapons to carry out seductions where and when appropriate.

The university Education stream was high in sporting emphasis and her growing physical prowess was observed by the Uni fraternity and resulted in closer attention and opportunities for acknowledgement and rewards.

University social functions were frequent, and the

expectation was that students would bring along a companion or partner. There was close watching of one another's body language and quiet observations and opinions formed.

Helen had become a regular companion of an attractive male student who was gay. Helen knew this, and they both had a lot of fun freely mixing with others during the evenings. They quietly laughed together when and if others tried to 'crack' their partnership when leaving at the end of such functions to go home. They laughingly admitted they felt comfortable because their favourite tune was, 'Save the last dance for me', often singing it together as they headed home together to sleep in their separate beds. Their own brand of humour added to their enjoyment of each other's company.

A more sinister relationship developed when one of the senior lecturers decided he wanted to add Helen to his long list of conquests.

The university students thought they were, and in fact were encouraged by some tutors to think of themselves as, pseudo-intellectuals. It could be great fun and added to the atmosphere at many parties and functions, particularly when they were so often joined by other university friends and colleagues. They all took pride on arranging and participating in what was generously referred to as 'an Australian Bacchanalian Orgy'. It was basically a drunken revelry. Quite some expertise was associated with these events, not the least being the choice of venue and the confidential nature of the list of participants. There was status of a kind attached to being included. This is when the 'pseudo' types really came into their own. It was expected that the event would proceed from after 11pm through to breakfast, at an 'as yet undecided' location. There were copious quantities of alcohol and limited drugs for those who knew where, how and from whom they could be procured. Canned music, or sometimes live music of varying quality, filled the evenings and the performances and quality of the renditions varied in the extreme.

Helen, by now well into the mid-term, had participated in a couple of these occasions, and one memorable romp took place at the home of a recently deceased aunt of a student in an inner-city suburb. Loud music and the occasional tuning into sport on TV as more loud background noise, and with the aid of alcohol, inhibitions were lowered. People were drunk and inclined to be amazed by a vivid description rendered by one of the so-called widely travelled 'student pseudos' of what was available in men's toilets in vending machines in the town of Halle, in northern Germany. There were many raucous interjections and encouragement to elaborate, so the provoked student went into full demonstration mode. Three products, he assured everyone in a loud voice and with an almost hysterical pose. Everyone yelling and screaming, "demonstration please!"

"OK. Mini vibrators, a pack of condoms with an illustrated phallus, and an in-English, 'Travel Pussy' brochure whose description also read 'Kunstliche Vagina'."

A not-quite-stunned silence was followed by loud demands for translation. So many apparently super-smart intellects offered comments showing the height of their young naivety and sense of the absurd. Once it had been established that it meant a c--- like vagina, the music and raucous comments moved on. It all seemed a bit weird and baffling to Helen, but as the evening progressed sexual partnerships were established and many then moved surreptitiously to darkened corners, bedrooms, toilets, chairs or just on the floor where coupling began and continued. It was a big 'rage' that pleased those who stayed on and depressed a small percentage who went home early — with a vow not to go again.

Late in the evening, and actually in the early hours of the Sunday morning, some behaviour exceeded common decency as two boys began opening cupboards and drawers looking for property that had belonged to the deceased aunt and throwing items around inviting the ghost to appear. Helen thought it very poor, immature behaviour from juvenile idiots, who would one day guide and teach the country's future generations. The behaviour lacked any sense of decency or humour. Helen had little or no humour within herself but still recoiled from the performance.

Helen by now had maturity of her own well in advance of her contemporaries and although she did indeed have sex with a fellow student that evening, it was a coolly thought through act with no intention of any relationship ensuing. Just a happening because of the circumstances. It could just as easily have been with a female but being bi or lesbian at the moment did not feature. Helen was becoming quite sexually experienced.

The learning program for the fledgling teachers marched on as the tutors continued to influence their pupils in subjects as wide-ranging as racial and sexual discrimination, religious motivations, verbal and physical bullying, while emphasising their own biases and bigotry along the way. Most of the teachers had a socialist political preference and favoured state-financed education systems. The most influential tutor for Helen was Matthew Coetzee, a senior lecturer who had decided that Helen was to be his next sexual conquest. To achieve that aim, he did his own version of stalking on campus and just 'accidentally' began running into her in corridors, entrance ways and sporting facilities. He was one of her regular tutors specialising in English. That also meant he regularly marked and assessed her work. The nodding acquaintance slowly grew into a more familiar and friendly greeting and a feeling of warmth.

However, if Matthew thought he was progressing well, he had badly underestimated Helen Murphy. She was more than happy to allow his advances to progress, and was very happy to receive disproportionately generous marks for assignments. She expressed her thanks to him and in response Matthew glibly replied, "I think I'm reasonably astute but 'Luck is preferable to brains and luck is a fickle mistress'!"

Helen was not quite sure if it was a subtle message about being a mistress. In more serious vein, Matthew liked to talk about human types. He told Helen he had categorised her as an 'F type' personality. Fanatical.

He was more correct than he realised about her extreme zeal. It provoked Helen to react a little carelessly back to him by suggesting he was a 'Y type'. A Yes Man. One who agreed with most opinions just to please. They agreed to disagree after much verbal jousting.

One evening Helen found herself accepting an invitation to a few drinks and supper at Matthew's apartment, driven by a single-minded urge to succeed at any cost even though she could imagine the conduct expected of her. Matthew had prepared well with lighting and soft music. He was an amusing host with plenty of stories about education and travel. Generous quantities of Shiraz were available as Helen had previously said she liked this type of wine.

The evening progressed well with plenty of opportunities for Helen to explore the apartment, and then for her to secrete some hidden equipment which she hoped would be utilised later. She didn't feel the least bit guilty about this as her obsessiveness over toxic masculinity encouraged her to act under the rationale of 'fair game', to stress her antagonism to what she perceived as misogynistic behaviour. She considered it to be merely counter action.

Slowly but surely Matthew's plan moved forward as the food, the alcohol and the ambience combined to achieve the relaxed atmosphere he wanted. The music had been chosen to create the opportunity to slowly dance bare-footed in the lounge in a soft warm embrace. That progressed to cuddles and contact of face and lips. Soft and intimate murmuring from Matthew accompanied the progress. Helen made no negative moves but just let the seduction develop. She quite admired his expertise; he was obviously well practised.

The tempo moved up a notch when Matthew suggested a move to the bedroom and then began to remove his clothes and suggested she do the same. The interior of the house was warm, as was the apparent situation. Now Matthew began to be all over her with less respect than previously shown. Roughly he pulled off her bra and panties as with his clothes all on the floor he flaunted his manhood with obvious pride, and even murmured, "How lucky you are!"

He was very expert as his lips caressed her upturned nipples and his fingers explored her genitalia feeling for her clitoris. Both these explorations gave Helen passing moments of pleasure as Matthew hurried on with his own pleasure and encouraged her to massage those parts of his body that pleasured him. He quickly forgot about her as he positively urged her to use digits and tongue to penetrate unusual orifices in different ways. There was absolutely no warmth or empathy in the activity and the moment he had ejaculated, the warm and friendly evening was over with hardly a farewell. The important things that Helen did gather up and place among her clothes were small audio and video recording units she had previously discreetly placed in the lounge and bedroom.

Next time they met, Matthew could hardly be bothered to pass the time of day with her, and any suggestion of favourable attention had gone up the chimney. In fact, Matthew now seemed to single her out for criticism. In one conversation with others, he was heard to use under his breath the word 'brazen' about her. That filtered back to Helen and was the motivation for her to start on her pay back plan.

Helen's next assignment was returned from Matthew with comments across the bottom: "Poor effort, more energy expected." Helen immediately challenged him directly in class and he said peremptorily, "come to my office at the end of this tutorial!" That followed, with Matthew beginning the conversation with a blunt opening, "The overgenerous treatment is over, you will now need to earn every single point awarded. Your penis envy and apparent physical superiority only highlights your vulnerability and jealousy, and covers up your lack of passion and skill."

"Wow!" exclaimed Helen, almost falling backwards under the head-on attack. She took several very deep and slow breaths as she recovered her equilibrium.

Sarcastically she responded using every ounce of calmness she could muster, "Well now, no thanks to you for your 'penny lecture' and the bitterness that seems to follow your apparent sexual triumph. It seems you enjoyed the evening even less than I did, but you are about to become the loser! You have just provided the catalyst for me."

This pronouncement was followed by a brief silence so Helen hurried on, "Do you want to hear the bad news?"

Still no reply, so Helen went into full flow. "You were not to know that amongst my various skills and know how acquired in my past life is a great ability in the use of audio-visual equipment. The sexual events last week in your apartment are good examples of the wonders of modern technology!"

The silence was broken by bluster as Matthew attempted to control the small involuntary movements of his hands, feet and facial expressions. A little dribble out of one corner of his mouth and one nostril betrayed his understanding of the mess he was in.

Helen had triumphed in her plan to 'kick male arse' and inflict hurt as she advanced through her new life. She also received excellent grades in her exams. A lesson she took to heart.

Helen's persona for the remainder of her university years seemed upbeat and chirpy, but also calm and friendly to the casual observer. In her own mind, she sometimes likened her role to Helen of Troy. As though there was an element of loyalty or even royalty in her role.

Matthew became a serious casualty as he was used by her to the nth degree and Helen was thus propelled up through all levels to graduate with top results. This enabled her to obtain a teaching role at a school of her choice and begin a career as a qualified and respected professional child educator; a schoolteacher respected by society in her mind.

There was not such a happy result for Matthew who was constrained by Helen's vindictive use of her evidence, and shortly before the end of Helen's final year, he finally resigned from the university after much personal anguish and suffering acute depression and the total disintegration of his sense of who he was.

5

Linda Alexander

Now a thirty-year-old career police officer with a growing reputation as a Detective Inspector, Linda seemed destined to continue moving up the ranks. She had done the hard yards as she had chosen to be on the side of law-abiding citizenship and society, after her parents had been motivated to seek a new life for the family in Australia; far away from what they had perceived to have been an unfair 'privileged' lifestyle in South Africa under apartheid rules. Almost straight into the Australian police force after attending university in Perth, Linda had been identified as a prospect for higher office. She loved being in the police force, and had matured as exposure to training and law breakers had widened her appreciation of the foibles and failings of human beings. Her appetite for challenge and experience was well met within the scope of police activities. On the social side, her sexual needs were adequately met within her non-obligatory relationship with Jeremy (a friend of her brother), which was cosy and friendly, but perhaps because of her having grown up in very privileged conditions in South Africa she was not seeking an overly supportive partner, nor at this stage a long-term partner and children so early in her life. Being a successful police officer fulfilled her current desires.

She well remembered a major 'blue' in her early police days when she willingly fell into a relationship with another police officer, and then was embarrassed to discover he was married, with no intention of changing his lifestyle to accommodate Helen into his life. There were plenty of alpha males in the police force but she had been lucky to be associated mainly with good guys who helped and encouraged her in her drive for enlightenment and personal knowledge.

An efficient DI was the image Linda presented. Displaying a smart manner and dress sense, it was easy to recognise a physically and mentally fit officer with a no-nonsense attitude enjoying her career status. All achieved by hard work and application. There was no room for inertia in her make-up. Conscientious, talented and honest was how she was described by colleagues.

Linda was a regular recipient of awards and recognition for her work but she had the knack of gaining these achievements without there being jealousy or envy from her team. The awards were valued, forgotten and moved on from. Well-hidden ambition drove her on to further her studies and to absorb the culture and education on offer. She was loyal, friendly and considerate to her co-workers. She was as popular as any regular Manager could achieve. 'Friendly but not friends' was her personal motto for all workmates. Associates and those close to her admired her for quality upbringing that had cultivated in her an unconscious professional courtesy and style. That, mixed with her 'never give up' attitude on problems, made her a formidable foe.

Whenever practical, Linda took a few days of sabbatical leave and went back to Perth in Western Australia, to visit her parents and an old school friend; mainly to recharge her 'batteries' and to try to remain in normal mode, to offset the inevitable heavy emphasis that police work and routine imposed on attitudes. She found the routine 'ordinariness' of the lifestyle enjoyed by her parents refreshed her inner being. Their community seemed very ordinary and safe; the whistle-blowing postman, the old-fashioned barber shop, the traditional milkshakes, cash refund bottles, manual gear-change cars, tea and scones ritual, and even courteous train conductors seemed to be current experiences that she remembered from childhood.

She recalled further back again, to fountain pens, blotters, ink wells and money buried in cakes. What is 'normal' or simply just passed on? Her relationship with her parents was important to her, and much of that stability was still enjoyed with her brother Brendan, the banker, transferred from a base in London and now domiciled in Melbourne. Linda shared with Brendan a modern apartment on the 16th floor of a complex at the top end of Collins Street, in East Melbourne. Very safe and convenient as they could both close up and go away individually or at the same time, and leave everything secure and tidy.

Linda particularly enjoyed her long and quiet discussions with her father John, a medical doctor, as he was super curious about her police work and the strange problems she had to cope with, particularly when they involved physical or mental abnormalities requiring special skills to remedy. With her mother Prue, a successful senior mining corporate executive, she loved to ring and tease her by saying, "Hi Mum, what's for supper?" and get the excited response, "Wonderful! Are you in Perth, darling?"

Her long-term partner, Jeremy, her brother's friend, was also a banker, and with whom Linda shared many confidences and sometimes secrets. Although Linda's parents knew of Jeremy — from both Linda and Brendan — it was significant that he had never been invited to Perth by Linda to meet them. Both parents were busily involved in their professional careers and with their own circle of friends in the environment they had chosen for themselves. They were immensely proud of both Brendan and Linda, and always aware of the underlying concern of threats that existed in police work. Linda tried to reassure them that as her rank rose the likelihood of personal damage retreated.

The suburb of Cottesloe in Perth was still 'home base' for Linda and had all the familiarity and pleasures she remembered from university years and her fledgling policing experiences. Her memories sustained her enthusiasm for her career, despite the odd blunder along the way. She had never fully confessed all of those to family or friends.

Back in Victoria, to stay fit and forceful, and on top of her game, Linda maintained both a tough physical and mental regime. It consisted of regular (at least three times a week) gym work carrying out a vigorous routine that was regularly assessed and upgraded by her personal trainer. There was also regular psychological skills training, through the three regular phases befitting a senior police officer to maximise the mental skills being developed. She thrived on the lifestyle and never considered she was missing out on the more frivolous relaxed lifestyle enjoyed by some of her contemporaries, nor was she envious of missing out on perhaps the 'wild side' of life.

6
'Weirdo'

Everyone knew he was 'different'.

Graham Williams grew up on a small farm within a two-hour drive of central Melbourne close to a town in Victoria called Anakie. His parents were considered 'normal enough' and could be best be described as marginally successful farmers, running mixed cattle and sheep and some vegetables on 150 acres. His father was of limited education, with old-fashioned ideas about both family aspirations and behaviour. Corporal punishment had been violently administered to both Graham and his brother — often out of proportion to the perceived misdemeanours on these occasions. Animals were treated cruelly when tempers were lost.

Older brother Malcom was robust enough to handle farm life and rough behaviour, with a thick skin and much emotional resilience. Graham, nicknamed 'Gussie' for some unknown or unremembered reason, was not so fortunate. His main support came from his grandmother who lived an hour away. They laughed together and played name games as 'Gussie and Grannie'.

Malcolm Williams, from the age of ten, was strong enough to help on the farm and thus be appreciated. Graham, two years younger, was a big contrast. He was small of stature but at the same time a roly-poly overweight kid. He was pale-skinned, with light-blue eyes, and wore round, silver-framed glasses. Malcolm was good at physical, contact sports — recognised by teachers and contemporaries as outstanding in sport. Their parents provided support to help his successes. In comparison, Graham had no such attributes, and in fact he disliked human contact. One talent he did have was an ability to play the piano. Self-taught on a beaten old piano in a spare room, with the help of an astute music teacher at school, by the time he was eleven he was close to being recognised as 'outstanding' in that field.

The brothers were good enough friends — Malcolm big and strong and inclined to handle most things with an attitude of 'rip-tear, shit and bust', Graham with almost excessive care and attention to detail. Malcolm always looked out for Graham when they attended functions or were at school together so there was no direct bullying, but as the boys matured Graham became more obviously overweight and the fatness in his upper legs made it impossible for him to run without the upper legs grotesquely rubbing together. Ugly comments from some kids did not go unheard.

Graham Williams was recognised at secondary college by the chemistry and biology masters because he seemed fascinated with these subjects. He liked to hang around to be given time to experiment with mixing chemicals and witness the reactions, and to look at insects, worms and small animals preserved in formaldehyde. Malcolm left school when only sixteen and went back to work on the family farm. He was welcomed by family and friends and initially was relaxed by the constant supervision and instruction from his father.

Graham was a good scholar and in spite of the bullying and constant verbal abuse, he studied hard and advanced through to acceptance into medical school at Melbourne University. Special support had been given by the science masters and the music master encouraging his piano skill. He had a rare ability and loved playing jazz as well.

However, as time moved on Malcolm became more irritated by his father — to the extent of having one of the sheds at the far end of the farm converted into a small, comfortable cottage for him to live in. A carport protected his vintage Morris Minor and work Toyota. Graham occasionally spent time at the cottage as the boys matured but they had no strong common interests.

At university, Graham studied hard and passed all the preliminary exams and particularly enjoyed human anatomy. He was fascinated by dissecting cadavers. His relaxation took the form of frequenting small bars and restaurants, even jazz clubs, where his piano playing attracted applause and a few free drinks. He was singularly sexually unattractive to both males and females of his own age group but became friendly with a 'muso' associate from a jazz club. It was almost an association of opposites. His name was Jack Finch. Known as 'Finchie'. Some Jamaican heritage made him look physically like a Yul

Brynner copy with a dark complexion, jet black slicked-down hair and the addition of a small dark moustache and sideburns. Finchie had a hawk-like face, with a long, hooked nose above small thin lips, and as part of his image, he dressed mainly in black. He looked either evil or strong according to the personal point of view. Recreational drugs were in common supply with cocaine and the milder variants, plus the full range of alcohol was always readily available. Finchie had an inner-city flat close to most action spots and gradually he and Graham (aka 'Gussie') exchanged confidences as they frequented similar venues together.

The many extracurricular activities for Gussie slowed his progression through his medical exams and to supplement his limited income, through connections he was lucky enough to be appointed as a part-time mortuary assistant. There was not a big queue wanting the job but Gussie found it attractive. He enjoyed dissecting cadavers, labelling and measuring intimate body parts. Various labels applied to the position. He learnt that a 'diener' was a morgue worker and that there was a career path available. The Melbourne morgue in Kavanagh Street, Southbank, was an easy walk from the CBD. By most people's definition, it was a macabre employment role.

Finchie was both wild looking yet very attractive to both male and female partners, but as it was obvious that he and Gussie were no more than musical associates and friends, they were labelled 'The Odd Couple' or 'Black and Fat Whitey'. After some time, Graham was invited to move into the flat with Finchie to share the costs, and with two separate bedrooms there was no conflict as they were just flatmates.

Finchie had no medical interest or wish to experience anything about the mortuary, and to all intents and purposes Gussie seemed asexual and almost certainly still a virgin. Finchie attracted more than his share of willing sexual partners of both genders and Gussie quickly learned to make himself absent from the major living end of the house and take to his room.

The music scene in Melbourne was friendly and co-operative for active, talented musicians such as the Odd Couple. Finchie had a wide range of contacts and obtained many gigs. Gussie also went along to play as and when he was available, and the pair's use of drugs such as ice, methadone and cocaine was common. Gussie was only an occasional purchaser, but Finchie was a regular user and sometimes a small distributor. Finchie had briefly introduced Gussie to his supplier, whom he called 'Ricky R'. He also referred to him as 'Rolls-Royce' — ostensibly because he was expensive and difficult to contact — but the real reason was to protect his anonymity. Ordering was always long-winded and involved a call to a burner phone. Ricky R was a mysterious person who perhaps could easily be underestimated as he seemed quiet, shy and well dressed; he was not at all 'showy'. He was always reliable and considered Finchie typical of the wild musical scene, and thought his occasional companion, the fat 'piano man', seemed weird.

In Graham's family, crumbling relationships over the past several years had deteriorated from poor into dismal. His father had gradually become more physically aggressive towards his wife and son Malcolm. Finally, Malcolm had rows with him, and amid serious acrimony left home saying he never wanted to see his father again. He emigrated to Canada. That turned out to be final. Not many years later their mother was killed in car crash on the way home from a CWA meeting. Probably the only serious mourners at the funeral were Graham (Gussie) and his maternal grandmother.

The father, as a widower, went into a self-destructive drive that everyone could see would have only one outcome. No one really cared because he had alienated his neighbours, he couldn't understand the lifestyle enjoyed by Gussie and had made no effort or compromise to be closer to either son. To him, Malcolm had gone AWOL and had deserted him. The inevitable death followed.

The will was a huge surprise as the estate was bigger than most would have predicted, and after several strange bequests the bulk was left to Gussie. A part of the will that caused much comment was an amount bequeathed to the RSPCA. It was totally out of character as their father had never treated his animals with any kindness or respect. There were no challenges to the will and probate was quickly confirmed. Gussie was immediately a wealthy man. He wasted no time establishing exactly what was now his, and it was more than expected; in bank accounts, shares, and collectibles. What a mean old bugger he turned out to be. Gussie was the main beneficiary but was sad not to have received the generosity in kind when his father had been alive. He set up initiatives to find his brother.

The farm was a mixture of quixotic strengths and weaknesses befitting the way in which their father had lived. Dreadful interior standards and quality of furniture, and hardly used farm equipment. Gussie set about a huge clean-up and a detailed inspection of all documents relating to the farm including the deeds and titles. The plan was to sell it all. He discovered that the two acres that housed the cottage that Malcolm had lived in before going overseas was actually on a separate title. Gussie decided to keep that for himself as a country retreat and took steps to renovate the property. He also kept the old Morris Minor that had through neglect seriously deteriorated. Maybe he could join a vintage car club. Quite normal thoughts!

His next not quite so normal thinking was a decision to exit medical school, much to the consternation of all the professors and tutors, as they regarded him as talented and even extraordinary. They counselled him to stay on but he was hell bent on pursuing a lifestyle in music. With the wealth he now had, he would do what he wanted. He began to wear more unconventional clothes, grew in confidence and even mastered how to summon a wine waiter with a mere sideways glance.

A new influence and passion was entering his life. In the 'music bubble' of late-night jazz club music, Gussie and Finchie were now recognised as talented musicians and often fawned over, mainly by female patrons. Like any normal male, Gussie often visualised a hot sexual relationship with someone he fancied. However, being very unattractive and totally sexually inexperienced, he knew such an outcome was nearly impossible, but his imagination allowed many fantastic scenarios.

One evening in the morgue, Gussie was attending to the partially naked body of a young woman who probably had been a prostitute and who had overdosed on drugs. His job was to prepare the body to assist the pathologist to identify the cause of death. Some touching and or moving of the body was involved. Gussie's mind wandered back to a female patron who the previous evening had been loud and conspicuous in shouting to 'The Piano Man' to never stop playing and to 'come and be my slave'. A blow-up adult-sized doll would have been more appropriate.

As he stood in the morgue looking at the body, he realised he had an erection and as he was alone, he masturbated guiltily through to ejaculation. What a release and what a high! On his next shift in anticipation, he carefully showered and added some makeup to his face. Disappointment that there was no such similar experience, just the routine setting up in preparation for the pathologist. However, a few days later a beautiful young part African woman awaited his cleaning and repair. She was extraordinary beautiful and voluptuous and Gussie leaned in closely to touch her black crinkly hair. His fingers tingled and without hesitation he bent over and kissed her soft lips. He rushed on to masturbate over her naked body.

Several previous forays by Gussie to recruit a sexual partner at a jazz evening had resulted in rough rebuttals. His capacity to freely supply drugs seemed to add no incentive for them to want to participate.

Gussie was well aware he was now straying into necrophilia. He was patently aware that psychiatrically he would need treatment, and professionally there would be no forgiveness for his actions.

7

Gussie on His Journey

Now in possession of inherited wealth, Gussie made a concerted effort to upgrade his cottage in the country, starting with a full paint job inside and out, garden upgraded, a new entrance gate with security, and driveway spruced up all made it very attractive. With an almost total internal makeover — new appliances, floor coverings, drapes and expertly selected furniture — a luxury holiday home in the country was created. This was to be a well-protected private residence equipped with appropriate security safeguards. Few people were aware of its existence and even fewer had ever been invited.

A carefully selected group of Finchie's 'cronies' were invited to a Saturday evening at the farm cottage, and with the incentive of a free flow of drugs, plenty of loud music, and free transport to and from the location, Gussie kept the address reasonably low key. Everyone had a great time and treated the premises with respect. Few of the partygoers could have detailed the address as they had been delivered in the dark and the homeward trip the next day was made by most in a bit of a stupor.

Buoyed by this first success, Gussie decided to try again to attract a partner to accommodate him sexually. He chose at random a sex worker called Lucille and enticed her, in the absence of Finchie, to the city flat where he plied her with quality cocaine in dust form. With her tiny little body, she was totally compliant and then she quickly passed out. He bundled her up, lifted her into the back seat of his Audi ute, and with great care not to be sighted by anyone, drove post-haste to his deserted farm at Anakie. He made doubly sure to park around the back of the house out of sight and then closed the front gates. Effortlessly, he lifted Lucille's light body into the back bedroom where he set about reviving her. He was confident in his mind that as she was such a 'nobody' in so many ways, her absence would go unnoticed. He was also confident she would never remember the car — brand or model or licence plate number. Gussie knew the circumstances that sexually set him off and was aware that he could not now go back.

Shortly after regaining consciousness in the cottage, Lucille revived to the point where she began whining, "where are we? I want to go home!" She quickly became aware that something was restraining her movements and when she tried to sit up, found she was held down. It dawned on her she was in big trouble. Her heart pounded and her lips and mouth were dry. She was sure she was about to be raped. Her brain clocked in and she tried to reassure herself that this could be survived. Trying to stay calm, she looked around as best she could and was horrified to see obscene photos clearly collected from pornographic publications stuck to all the doors and windows. Her confidence about survival disappeared. She did not know or recognise her captor, so was unable to call his name and beg for help or release. He was unrecognisable as he now wore a surgical mask and had his hair pulled back in a ponytail.

He suddenly was right there beside her and gently asked, "How are you now?"

She screamed and yelled in hysteria and gave Gussie a real fright. His pale blue eyes peered closely into her face and after a few moments — as he rubbed his gums with heroin — he enquired in a most reasonable fashion if he could interest her in joining him?

That set off another hysterical tirade from Lucille who, being very frightened, punctuated it with a variety of four-letter adjectives asking him, "Are you aware who my uncle is?"

She went on to demand, "Let me go! He will see you in jail for this!"

The only response was, "Oh, yeah, yeah!" from Gussie as he began to strip off the remainder of her clothes and to push and poke at parts of her anatomy.

A wave of terror swept through her now wholly naked body as Gussie opened what looked like a toolbox holding a range of medical equipment. Simultaneously he took from a smaller container a range of drugs, such as ice and methadone. In a very strange, almost demented way, he initially tried to hold a conversation with Lucille as he examined her body, without any obvious intent as yet to physically violate or damage her.

But she was extremely hysterical and could not formulate any coherent comments.

Gussie, tiring of the one-sided conversation, eventually administered what he thought would be an effective mix of drugs to make her more compliant and quieter. She seemed to take the lethal mix well and even smiled and murmured thanks for a brief moment, before descending into deep unconsciousness. And then she died.

Now Gussie began to think of himself as 'Gus' — the more mature person in charge of his own destiny! He closely inspected his new beautiful female friend who lay there so compliant and quiet, with not a negative word to say. As he busied himself around the room and house, over time she seemed to him to gradually change into a beautiful, almost translucent, shade of white. His activities seemed to be suspended in time to him, as he looked closely at room ornaments, slowly cleaned and tidied the house and swallowed more drugs — a couple of buprenorphine, supplemented with a snort of cocaine. He was ready! Gus gently kissed Lucille on the lips, intimately touched most parts of her uncovered naked body and then progressed as he fancied with fondling, digital and vaginal penetration and facial violence.

Much later as reality settled in, he became aware of the intruding odour and the need to dispose of the body in a concealed manner. He had prepared for this, and now bundled the body into a plastic bin liner that he securely tightly, and followed that with a second equally tightly tied liner. It was a challenge to bundle the parcel into the ute and an even bigger challenge to think where to dispose of it. His final decision was to wait until the early hours of the morning, when the streets were close to deserted, and then drive up one of the small lanes off Bourke Street in Melbourne, where he unceremoniously dumped Lucille's body into a large skip bin. He was sure he was not observed and he had deliberately muddied his car registration plates. He waited until first light to go home to his shared flat with Finchie, who had not even noticed his absence.

Gus was relieved to find no one commenting about his current activities or anyone with any apparent interest in him.

A month later, Gussie was to do a jazz gig in Geelong, unaccompanied by Finchie. This suited them both as Finchie did not want to go so far away and Gus assured him he was happy to arrange his own accommodation. What an opportunity to further his new mature identity!

The jazz gig did not begin until around 11.30pm, in a low-key fashion, and Gussie was applauded generously for his wonderful piano interpretations of the saxophone and violin. Earlier on Gus had tried to hit on a heavily made-up female he was sure was a prostitute.

She succinctly told him, "Piss off Ugly!"

Not totally put off, and as the evening wore on and drugs filtered through the audience, Gus believed people would begin to see things through rose-tinted glasses. He was right, and about 4am she accepted his invitation to visit his 'country home'. She was not at all worried and both of them a little befuddled by drugs, they entered the front door into the neat and tidy cottage, fresh smelling, air conditioned and cold. Visible was a desk, a computer, and lounge chairs. Gus hurriedly turned on the heating and offered her more drugs as he had earlier promised.

Expertly he reassured her as she kept asking befuddled but consistent questions, "Yes, yes, you can stay as long as you want, even stay forever! I'll take care of you!" He was not disconcerted by her questions, "What's in there? Where is the toilet?"

He offered to show her around or take her outside for fresh air until he got tired of the charade. Then he moved with surprising speed and efficiency, gave her the lethal drug mix to terminate her life and followed with what now seemed to him like a practised personal sexual routine of fondling, sex and violence. Even the matter of disposing of the body did not worry him — he had apparently been very successful the last time so he copied the method.

Melbourne Central Police Station

Melbourne Central Police Station. Duty Sergeant to some of his new constables: "You will never guess what the latest case is!"

"Go on then, surprise us," responded one.

In hushed tones the Sergeant droned, "A wrapped up female body found encased in bin liners in the CBD."

That received startled looks and a tirade of questions, and the Sergeant went on to add a few facts: "She is small, been dead for some days, been smacked around a few times, beautifully made up, and clearly sexually assaulted in a variety of ways."

There were questions galore as the staff members clamoured for more information. The questioning was broken up by the arrival of specialists and senior personnel from Pathology and Forensic Science departments. Notification had already been sent to the Coroner's Court. Such a discovery set all the wheels of the police station into high speed as responsibilities and jobs were allocated. The incident was fully recorded so higher ranks would have noted the discovery.

The first job was to identify the victim, and it was clear that this would take time. No clothes, no jewellery, and no outstanding marks or features. She was a tiny little cadaver and it was hard to estimate just how old she was. The forensic scientist and pathologist began all the necessary DNA steps, collecting samples of every minuscule deposit anywhere on the body or wrappings. There was particular interest in hair and the contents of a condom.

The only real comment exchanged between the early examiners through their masks was, "Clearly the work of a necrophiliac. A sick bastard who needs to be caught."

They went on to comment on the all-pervading smell. They were well aware of how long it would linger. All the skills and resources of haematology and spectrometry would be added into the research that would be energetic. This crime was disgusting.

The Inspector allocated to the crime was efficient, assembled his resources quickly, and was an excellent communicator to all team members.

The first question was, who was the victim? No-one fitting the description had been posted as a missing person, an under-age child, or a known sex worker. Possibilities on the identity of the perpetrator wandered far and wide. Members of the medical profession were high on the list because of the necessity to treat and handle a human body.

The initial DNA enquiries, despite the diligence applied, turned up no positive identification. More general and broad enquiries amongst known sex workers seemed to be homing in on a tiny woman known to frequent pizza joints and the Friday night casual music scene. She was not posted as missing but had not been spotted for a few weeks. She had no known close associates and was thought to maybe be from the country or outer suburbia.

Ten days after the discovery of the well-wrapped body in the skip bin, a call came through to Melbourne Central Police Station begging for an inspection be made of a collection of rubbish bins from which an "unimaginable stench" was emanating.

The first police response was, "That sounds like a council matter."

The almost hysterical shout in reply was, "Sounds like bloody nothing! It stinks, get someone there, urgently, and fix it!"

Council and police arrived simultaneously and agreed the smell was revolting. On opening the bin cover, it was even worse, and jammed in the bin was what turned out to be a decaying body wrapped in tightly tied bin liners.

Exclamations ranged from, "Oh, my God" to "Bloody hell" and a range of bolder expletives.

News of the horrific discovery spread like lightning through the police force, council authorities, and to the media. It quickly became referred to as, 'The Twin Bins' murders. The police now had high-profile serial murders to deal with.

As in the earlier discovery, the body was female, death some days previously, but significant facial makeup could still be seen, along with clear signs of sexual activity and some bruising. Neither very young nor very old, of average size — and possibly a sex worker? The person disposing of the body must have been at least of medium strength.

This posed for the police team a fresh DNA challenge. Who was she? Another challenge for the police was the clear need to upgrade the level of their inquiry, and in short time the Assistant Commissioner — in consultation with his senior colleagues — appointed his newly promoted Detective Inspector Linda Alexander to head the investigation. Part of his arriving at the decision to appoint Linda was the profile she had earned by solving a complicated double murder that had transcended state borders and various criminal genres. She was respected as a detective with an ability to communicate her leadership to a broad team. This case was going to be a challenge, all the way down to keeping the public informed but not fearful. However some delicate meetings were necessary within the force to minimise any discontent over the appointment of Linda Alexander to this important investigation.

9

'Twin Bins' Investigation and Arrest

For Linda Alexander, the first step was easy as, having been appointed as the Case Inspector with everyone's approval, she requested a move to allow her full control to select her own team. In the allocated incident room; equipped with full communication systems, tables, chairs, files, cabinets and whiteboards, plus a separate clerical staff member available 24 hours per day, Linda now began to recruit her own team. When that was finalised, she summarised the current situation to them, beginning with an analysis of 'What is known and what is unknown?'

The 'Knowns': two dead, as yet unidentified, young women, perhaps sex workers, not yet reported as missing but probably Melburnians. Reasonably healthy, both of whom had very heavy, well-applied facial makeup still on. Both cadavers had recently experienced sexual penetration but not violent to a level of damage. Some bruising to face, lips and nipples. Both had dyed head hair but not pubic hair. Opinion was that consistent with appearance they had been used by a necrophiliac.

The 'Unknowns': Identities — the victims, and the perpetrator or perpetrators.

Both a massive concentration and speed were requested from the forensic science department. The media was asked to help to find out about missing family, friends or associates. Where would these young women frequent? Police undercover agents were asked to enquire from known controllers of female escort agencies.

It did not take long for a report of a missing co-worker from a central city location to come in. She was Kelly McPherson, a known drug user, extremely small in stature, known for her cheery nature and big smile. A large mole on her right shoulder and a tattoo of a poodle on her left ankle were spoken of. No known address but often shared accommodation with another street girl who sometimes worked similar locations. So, she was identified as a prostitute. No help was forthcoming about likely companions or users over the immediate past.

Linda was keen to build the enthusiasm and culture in her team so in her first Incident Room meeting she was complimentary on the team's early success in identifying victim number one, and stressed the need to dig deeper into connections for more leads. She also stressed urgency in attempting to visualise a candidate for the murderer, and theorised aloud possibilities, inviting input from the growing team.

She asked, "Well, what do you think we have here? Young, old, twisted, or totally unremarkable; special handicaps or talent? Do you think it's a male or female perpetrator?" She stopped there and waited for responses. Only one came without prodding.

Senior Constable Beth Jenkins offered, "Definitely a man in my opinion. No woman would be that perverted!"

Linda gently agreed, but said that statistically there has been the odd example.

Still trying to thought-provoke the team she went on, "What experience or skills would be needed, even to tolerate the smell? Cosmetic training, medical qualifications or even abattoir experience? What about in a morgue? Are heavy drug users more prone to ugly involvements; known paedophiles?"

Responses became more spontaneous and even ridiculous, and voices were raised. Linda felt team participation had begun. She had no experience in necrophilia but knew they needed to flush out some possible culprits or connections. She asked the team to try to agree on the most likely category of suspects. Many hours later the shortened list, not in merit order, came together. Someone with medical training, a loner, physically unattractive but quite strong, under 50 years of age, mortuary experience, and personally very tidy.

Details of the second victim came in and she was identified as a prostitute, drug user, from around the Geelong, Ballarat, Bendigo areas, known to hang around nightclubs and the jazz scene. She had been missed by associates but was reputed to go on the occasional bender and disappear for a day or two. She was identified as Lucille Black by a cousin from the same area and profession. The police had inspected a Geelong jazz venue which by reputation had a bad name. It was very ordinary in appearance, as was the quality of the music presentation. The venue was characterised by an plain street frontage, not on the main street, bright lights, well-built door man/bouncer and loud music drifting out the doorway. It was just bad luck that Lucille had chosen to ply her trade on that night.

Quickly, the two victims had been identified. Where was the connection to the murderer? Someone or some surveillance equipment must have seen a car or van delivering the bodies to the rubbish bins in central Melbourne. But it seemed the answer was no.

Who could be a central Melbourne resident with such a secret habit and identity? DI Alexander needed to find out and arrest the very dangerous person before there were any more casualties.

The police team concentrated on the areas that could be examined through known data. Failed or deregistered doctors. Mortuary assistants who may have been dismissed for inappropriate behaviour, any known deviant sex/drug users. A comprehensive group but in some categories very vague. A more rewarding and forthcoming group were the street prostitutes, questioned about any strange or 'weird' men who regularly used their services. Other attempts to find a suspect were wide-ranging, and included speaking to all central cosmetic clinics specialising in injectables, staff working in abortion clinics, and the controllers 'in known brothels of call girls with a drug dependency. Much data to process and sort through looking for any possible leads.

The pressure brought to bear was wide and ceaseless. Linda led from the front, continually cajoling her team to dig deeper, as she indeed did herself. The team respected her as she respected them with praise, and often turned up with surprises of bagels and coffee as exhaustion started to set in. She had been successful in recruiting into her team Senior Constable Beth Jenkins from the Macedon Ranges area. They had worked together on a previous major inquiry, and although of different rank, experience and seniority, had become trusted friends and associates. Intuitively, Linda thought Beth would add urgency to the inquiry.

The added responsibility of providing regular updates to the media increased Linda's fatigue but also increased her profile. Other senior officers were more than happy to allow Linda the exposure.

As anticipated, after many days and unending pressure, a tiny lead surfaced. Through an almost casual comment it was reported that a part-time morgue assistant had not recently been to work. Not that that in itself was so unusual, as he had always been a bit irregular, but he was also described as 'different'. Ensuring that nothing was to be overlooked, and although marked as not particularly urgent, a follow-up provided a name and address of an inner-city apartment building. Linda instructed one of her detective sergeants to call at the premises. There was nothing greatly unusual to see when he was greeted at the door of the flat by Jack Finch looking his usual self, dressed in all black.

The polite police inquiry as to whether he worked in a

morgue made him laugh out loud and he questioned, "Do you think I could?"

The detective answered seriously, "this is no laughing matter, sir, but we have been given this address of such an employee."

Jack Finch did not look surprised but said, "Well, I don't but my friend does, but I don't think he works much at that these days, as we are co-musicians and mainly work in evening music gigs now."

The DS noted all that down, and then asked who Jack was referring to, and also if he could have a quick look around inside the apartment. Jack told him his friend's name and responded to the look around question with, "No problem at all, it's very small as there are only the two bedrooms."

That was all easily confirmed, and his answer of 'no' as to whether they had any extra accommodation in the city was noted as well.

Back in the incident room with this latest information, the atmosphere was buzzing. Was this a lead to 'The Person?' The resulting urgent deep dive into the personal data and background of Graham Williams gave everyone a surprise.

Linda immediately consulted with her boss who advised her on the need for confidentiality, and to proceed with caution and secrecy. Particularly with Jack Finch perhaps spreading excitement. Timing was now of the essence.

Within the incident room, the label 'the Fat Little Fucker' (the FLF) seemed to have arisen. Originally heard from a nightclub colleague of Jack Finch's, who had apparently burst out with it when an undercover officer had asked around about the Black and White musical duo. Another acquaintance had offered gratuitously, "Isn't he a deregistered doctor?" Who needs friends!

The forensic scientists, pathologists and psychiatrists were now worrying as to whether the perpetrator may be planning another kill as time went by. As it happened, Gus was getting the 'itch' to try again. Finchie had reported to him the 'mild' police enquiry without any alarm bells being raised.

Linda and her team and the higher ranks discussed apprehending Finchie for knowledge, information, and suspicion by extension. It was decided to wait a day as more data and information was being accumulated about 'Gussie' and his history. The hesitation turned out to be of value, as information was flowing in from many sources and when all put together revealed an overall picture of a tormented man.

Firstly, the strange partnership and relationship with Jack Finch. Jack turned out to be almost totally blameless in spite of playing in music gigs together with Gus over many years. He was the only friend and close associate that Gus had.

The best explanation Jack could come up with was, "I knew he was different but we clicked beautifully with our music, and we just came and went as we chose." But that was later.

The medical school records were interesting, showing a star pupil with no friends or associates.

The inherited wealth that helped Gus's decision not to complete medicine, and the purchase of an Audi SUV all helped to inform the overall picture of Gus Williams. It was easy to discover that the SUV was regularly parked around the corner from the city flat in a rented garage. From the time of purchase the car was Gus's pride and joy that he treated with infinite care and attention. He was totally enthralled with all the wonderful add-ons that had been sold to him; the leather-upholstered heated seats, the reverse cameras and the gap-maintaining safety features which he was proud to point out to all and sundry.

The SUV was not difficult to locate, obtain a warrant for, and then break into without notice, to vacuum the entire interior to pick up fine dust, hair and dirt which was urgently sent for forensic analysis and hopefully some connection to the dead women.

Upon subtle questioning, no one reported any unusual use or habits associated with the SUV. The locals knew Gus and Jack Finch were musicians and kept late and inconsistent hours. Occasional female company had been seen, but that was mainly with Jack.

The property at Anakie was easy to find, so Linda sent DC Beth Jenkins out to scout around and make enquiries in Geelong amongst the jazz music scene and street girls there. 'Gus and Finchie' were well known and musically respected, Gus for his outstanding piano interpretations. He was also known as ugly — unattractive, and quite different.

The pieces all added up and Linda applied for a search warrant for the premises at Anakie. This was granted without fuss on the evidence presented. All this time Gus Williams had been kept under surveillance and had not done anything untoward. Apparently Finchie had not alarmed him, nor had he sought further pleasure.

Without much fuss, but with all the regulatory witnesses, the search warrant was carried out using enough manpower to break in effectively. What a surprise — an immaculately clean and excessively tidy place, extremely fresh smelling. That was until forced entry was made into what looked like a fourth bedroom from the exterior, but was locked. This was another large, very clean room but with a faint, unusual smell. It had a large flat table in the middle, and a very large mirror on one wall entirely covered in pornographic photos and lewd illustrations. The biggest surprise was the massive refrigeration unit in the room.

The forensic team now swarmed all over the whole property and many commented on the immaculate state of the facilities.

Linda and her team now knew exactly where Graham Williams was at any time of the day or night, having established a 24/7 surveillance team on him. They found out he regularly ate his evening meal at an upmarket mid-city restaurant called La Boheme where he was known and treated with great respect. They even knew his favourite glass of wine. He did not drink to excess. Afterwards he sometimes went to the Green Parrot Snooker Parlour where he climbed carefully down the green stairs to enjoy a casual game. He was probably known as a regular but not as a musician and was left alone. He was described as a 'loner'.

The resources available to Linda and her team were formidable. The sophisticated listening and tracking equipment became more and more intrusive; the locking in on individual or group communications meant being able to hear and record information from every direction and to pinpoint the physical location almost down to the metre and the minute and hour. Then there was a requirement for specialists and their equipment to be available to interpret the data being built up that aided the certainty of guilt.

DI Linda Alexander, as the Officer in Charge of the investigation, had to request approval from the Superintendent to arrest Graham Williams. All evidence had to be produced and the correct procedures implemented. Linda found this challenging but enjoyed the logic and necessity. The Super was absolutely delighted about the speedy result and arrest, and conducted the media announcement and congratulations to his 'team'. Although he was brief, he was generous to his officers and for the co-operation received from the public. He directed enquiries down to his Inspector, and personally named DI Linda Alexander and her entire team as 'special'.

The media were like sharks in a feeding pond, and Linda was experiencing another step in her career. The newspapers had a field day, speculating about medical-type professionals indulging in obtuse activities with dead bodies beyond normal behaviour. Linda took it all in her stride, and wondered if she would ever have enough time to vigorously pursue the MBA that she was intent on doing.

The arrest went without incident as Gus clearly understood he was guilty. He knew his days of freedom were over for a long time and also understood the need for special medical and psychological treatment to be applied to him. The actual arrest was supervised by Linda, accompanied by a Senior Sergeant who carried out the formal procedure in the city flat. Although no physical reluctance was anticipated or encountered, two uniformed constables also waited outside the flat's front door.

Jack Finch was initially present, but quickly made himself scarce, saying only, "See you later!"

It was a great occasion for celebration, so Linda invited her partner Jeremy, her brother Brendan and his partner, plus DS Beth Jenkins and her husband, as her guests to an up-market dinner at Di Stasio's Citta restaurant in Spring Street, Melbourne.

This was a very rare event as Linda was regarded as emotionally and financially very conservative. Somehow, an alert photographer got a shot of them all and it was published in the Herald Sun newspaper, with an accompanying headline, "Master stroke solution to 'Twin Bins' mystery" There were two columns of congratulations and background story from the crime reporter. Congratulations flowed in from friends, family and associates. There was no real harm done but Linda was a little angry at the personal exposure. Her superiors were not unhappy, as it added to the overall good PR for the speedy solution of a major crime that had appalled the public.

10

Helen Murphy

Someone who also noted the police event, outcome and corresponding publicity was now successful school teacher, Helen Murphy. She read it all avidly and was full of admiration and envy.

To all intents and purposes, Helen was now in the middle of a solid career path to success that she had fashioned out from under a heavy load of a dreadful childhood involving mental and physical mistreatment. The recognition and respect she had earned to date as a middle seniority teacher, and now as a deputy principal, was due to her conscientious attention to everything that would support her drive for success. She was smart enough to camouflage the most blatant steps in pursuing her goals, of either stepping on other people or sabotaging their gains for her own ends, on her pathway upwards.

Helen was very good at her job and always put in the extra few yards to be appreciated, and was always the first to volunteer in her work as well as in the community, e.g. the

SES, CFA, parent teacher groups, Rotary or Lions Clubs, the Botanical Gardens or Council-community committees, or assisting at events on behalf of the school. Her list of outside qualifications and interests included passing the exams of the Australian Institute of Company Directors, which had involved significant study, to become a graduate of the Institute, and also completing a Grad. Diploma in Strategies and Management. She was contemplating doing a further business degree.

She presented as 'ever-helpful Helen', and received many awards and certificates for her contributions. The kids she taught 'sort of' liked her. She was not warm enough for them to actually 'love her' but she won over the hearts of many parents and grandparents by knowing and asking after them all by name.

Helen now shared an apartment in Brunswick, an inner northern Melbourne suburb, with an associate, who was also a school teacher but, by virtue of being younger than Helen and working in the Catholic school system, was in no way any competition or threat to Helen. They were able to share stories with no rivalry or conflict of interest, but were not real friends. At home, Helen was dominant, constantly challenging statements or opinions, but was smart enough to seldom go out on a limb to create a crisis. She recognised her power and privilege in the relationship. Both within the personal relationship at home and her professional career she was renowned for always being available to try anything and to attend anything to build her profile. The slightly snide comment made was, "she would attend the opening of an envelope".

More formidable was Helen's argumentative attitude over things that were in any way slightly intellectual; it seemed she wanted to illustrate just how smart she was to all and sundry. Her flatmate was also aware of the hero-worship syndrome Helen had for high-profile successful career females who regularly made the news and were photographed in the media.

A well-remembered verbal conflict at Helen's second-to-latest school had taken place in the teacher's lunch room, where there had been a discussion about the word 'soliloquy'. The word arose because the school was to present a small play in which a child actor expressed some thoughts about it. Debate started about how to spell soliloquy, then how to pronounce it.

Was it 'Sol LILL li quee'? or pronounced with the emphasis on the first syllable, like 'monologue'? Could it be used in the opening or the end of the play? Several of the teachers offered opinions, some were correct and some not. Helen took over and was in her element as she vigorously, with an element of superiority, put everyone right. She pointed out that it really meant, 'talking to oneself'. That was not the end of it, as she questioned the teacher in charge of the drama as to whether or not the presentation should proceed. Voices and temperatures rose dramatically and the skirmish had to stop so classes could begin. There was no solution but an outcome was arrived at when the principal 'rescued' Helen. This had happened before with contentious situations because the principal recognised and defended Helen's ability and talent. The principal herself had recognised that strong daughters were often the product of unusual childhoods, or perhaps a father giving preference to the daughter over a son who possibly preferred books to the outdoors, with a well-buried inner personality. This was not quite the case for Helen, but being rescued and thus clearly respected did help Helen to learn to restrain the nasty side of her personality and her relentless drive to question and challenge just about everything.

11
More of Helen's Journey

The very profile that Helen Murphy aspired to emulate evolved as the publicity around the successful arrest by Linda in the notorious 'Twin Bins' murder continued for weeks.

Helen resolved to herself, I'd like to be like her; I will be like her!

With a full-on push, she sourced from police recruiting information the steps and qualifications necessary to become a police officer. The B. Ed degree she had already obtained and a special category for mature recruits were advantages. She swung into action and in her usual style, researched every avenue and full details of the who's who of the most influential people to speed an application through to becoming a detective constable. Was there some form of apprenticeship?

Armed with every possible piece of useful data, Helen resigned from the Victorian education department with full recognition of awards and certificates. Perhaps a little prematurely, but with full confidence after all her preparation, she homed in on Victoria Police in spite of being tempted to apply to the Federal Police. She wanted to be in the Victoria Police which had minor variations from other forces. She worked her way through all the application steps, i.e. eligibility criteria, application, physical assessment and competency interview, various written and briefing exercises, and many medical and fitness tests.

She was relieved to discover the police force welcomed applications from people even in their mid-50s, even though compulsory retirement in most forces was sixty years of age. Being Helen, it was better still, because as soon as she was able to establish a meeting with a member of the recruiting personnel, her confident and winning personality and strong supporting documents resulted in positive responses.

Helen was aware of her narcissistic characteristics. Her studies confirmed that it was roughly a 1 in 100 trait, and that it gave a deep sense of self-importance that needed excessive admiration. Another trait was an indifference to hurting others, i.e. no empathy, and little awareness of the attitude of fairness. However, anxiety about her current or past behaviour was not in Helen's psyche. She was able to control and mask most such characteristics, and general police recruiting did not discover evidence of any overriding feature.

Helen was informed the application would take about six months. The long timeframe seemed to be because she had expressed an interest in Scientology. She had always found that people of reasonable intellect loved to debate; Christianity versus atheism and agnostic views, and with Scientology in particular. It gave her a personal platform. She was always on the lookout for subjects in which she could illustrate her superiority and in which she could challenge other opinions, and be argumentative.

Her knowledge of Scientology was quite deep. Many people took exception to the idea that it called itself a church. Created by an American called L. Ron Hubbard, it had beliefs described as a religion, defined by some as a cult, and others simply as a business. The Church of Scientology preaches that people are immortal spiritual beings who may have lost their way and the Church believes it has plenty of mythology to aid the repair work. A very big step to commit to full involvement. Many people have a small or passing interest in Scientology but Helen had always found it fascinating and a wonderful subject to liven up discussions. Quite an accelerant! Most people had enough knowledge to argue over 'atheist versus agnostic' and the spiritual differences, but Helen always tried to keep some ammunition up her sleeve and if all else failed to be provocative, she would then revert to the subject of reincarnation as it could cross over Scientology, Christianity and a multitude of other religions.

Helen used this knowledge to illustrate her intellectual arrogance by regularly challenging opinions on almost any subject. She insisted on explanations of opinions and would intrude even in people's vocabulary. No wonder some of her associates worked out a plan to avoid her. She knew full well the old adage around being a good listener to be liked, but chose to ignore it. It had become a well-rehearsed habit to take the opportunity to interrupt a conversation when someone was talking about something that gave them pleasure. Helen liked to interrupt with a challenge or a negative. She was skilful in her timing and adept as a killjoy. She was wise enough to pick her intrusion carefully. It was more than a childish game of tit for tat for her: Helen was an enjoyment spoiler.

Her training through the police academy advanced quickly as some of the powers that be had noted her application and it fitted the category the force was keen to promote i.e. talented younger women destined for higher ranks.

At an official function in one of the reception rooms in the new head office, Helen, as a new trainee, was invited to attend a presentation to a senior officer of a bravery award and long-service medal. There were thirty-five officers present in full uniform. It was a formal and traditional occasion to be followed by a less formal afternoon tea and refreshments.

Helen was excited to note that DI Linda Alexander was seated in the front row, and she waited impatiently for the formalities to conclude. With a cup of tea in one hand, Helen moved forward to give herself the opportunity to introduce herself to Linda.

Of course, Linda had heard about the brash young female trainee who had proclaimed, "I want to be like her!" In typical fashion Linda had never acknowledged to anyone that she was aware of the statement. Helen was clearly pleased to be talking to Linda and acquitted herself well with casual chit-chat by asking what current case the DI was working on? Linda briefly indicated the new challenge that organised crime was presenting with its sophisticated communications, encrypted devices, hiding techniques, and speed of transportation. Helen's day was made, and her enthusiasm was given another lift. Regretfully, what Helen had not observed or noted was the interpersonal skills that Linda illustrated on most occasions that allowed her to listen well, and then lead with consummate ease.

12
More of Linda Alexander

Now promoted to Detective Chief Inspector, Linda Alexander was a police officer on a serious upward career path through the Victorian police force. She loved being a police officer and all it stood for. She was serious in her endeavours both inside and outside her career. Some friends speculated that now in her 30s she may be missing out on one part of life's fulfilment? Linda did not countenance that. Off duty she was fully occupied with physical training and exercise through pilates and jogging which she loved, coffee meetings, especially with old friend Beth Jenkins who was now combining baby and career, her brother Brendan and his associates, and also pursuing her own personal development by undertaking an MBA degree and reading widely on many subjects. Linda had physical and mental challenges as she was nearing the completion of her MBA studies.

Her motto was just the same as her father used to say to her when she was a child, "We shall see what we shall see!"

Linda often hoped that in her new police role she may again share activities with Beth, as she really enjoyed the casual female chit-chat, without responsibility, with a friend she could trust.

Her new in-force project, which she was delighted to lead, was to head up a special taskforce created to concentrate on organised crime syndicates, to be called OCS. This was to be based at 313 Spencer Street, Melbourne. A major reason for her appointment was the success she had had in concluding the earlier case in the Macedon Ranges, outside Melbourne, known as 'The Terrible Twins' case, which featured two criminals later labelled as Mr Bigs. One was based in Adelaide, and the other co-ordinated from Sydney. They had used heavily encrypted communications. One of the 'bosses' was still at large and unidentified.

It was acknowledged that the Australian Federal Police (AFP) was well advanced in the battle against organised crime groups and the various ongoing connections and ramifications with bikies, drug traffickers, sex trafficking rings, burglary and currency thefts, guns, ammunition, prostitution and high-tech theft. One of the most lucrative was dealing directly in illegal drug importation and distribution; including cocaine, MDMA, methamphetamine, ketamine, cannabis and steroids. Many of the various activities overlapped between gangs.

For Linda, this meant a series of new terms entered into her vocabulary; including digital scientists, attribute device ownership, and imagery geometrics. As part of the new team-building, an Inspector was added to her division. Ian McDonald was an officer from the Western Division 5 area who was known and respected by Linda, as they had worked together in the past, and a colleague she knew she could rely on.

This new role was also a strategic appointment as part of broadening Linda's experience. Being a senior police officer was not without emotional wear and tear, and a facade had gradually grown around her public appearances. She was sometimes tired and grumpy, but that face she left at home. The appearance that was on show to colleagues, media and criminals was always confident, wise and open for discussions. Like most people she was frightened about lack of success and making mistakes. However, she always managed to tuck those fears away and press on confidently with the challenge in hand. Her low-key natural charm and humility were her greatest assets.

It was also announced that Linda was given an additional role to exchange information and data with the New Zealand Police in Auckland, as they were facing increased organised crime both internally and from overseas. This was envisaged as a short stint (maximum of four to six months) to be part-time in Auckland, to increase the exchange of information, speed up communication and increase co-operation.

Linda immediately arranged to meet with Inspector Ian McDonald for informal, weekly, 'away from the station' morning coffees, to build the relationship that she considered imperative. As soon as he had been appointed, she telephoned to invite him. He was delighted, as he was with her first comment over coffee of, "I hope you are OK with me calling you Ian, as

I am with you calling me Linda on private occasions."

That was a good start on what turned out to be a long and successful relationship. It was a getting to know you meeting, and a chance to get on the same page in the new division. They laughed and relaxed about how they needed 'to think like a crook' and, even more, they needed to train themselves to think like organised criminals. Ian adopted the use of the term 'Boss' to her in public discussions that allowed others to see the happy empathy.

Organised crime was described as an adults' fortune-making game of hide and seek, in which innocent bystanders can get badly hurt. The Division had emphasis on the utilisation of high-tech resources including drones and ROVs (remotely operated underwater surveillance vehicles.)

The need for close association with science and technology introduced regular interchanges with digital and forensic scientists. The 'Ninjas of forensics' as they were called, were a new group of specialists for Linda. This was all part of the learning curve for her and for her new support Inspector, Ian. They learned about the expertise of the imagery and geometrics team within the division, and the use of satellites and image processing.

An early opportunity to test the new team was provided by a prostitution/drug running scam in the Melbourne suburbs of Newport/Williamstown. The old port area was considered a smugglers' delight because of its history and the proximity of rail and derelict boating properties. It all started one quiet Sunday evening with a call to the Williamstown Police Station from a member of the public reporting two scantily clad young girls behaving erratically; either lost or drunk, wandering along Melbourne Road. The caller was a bit vague, saying it was close to Osborne Road, or maybe Station Road. The officer taking the call deemed it not urgent but noted it for follow-up. It was almost an hour later when a regular police patrol car went for a look. Two very young Asian girls were found in distress in Kororoit Creek Road, huddled in a dark corner and illustrated much fear as the police approached them. The officers attempted a conversation but it seemed the girls could not speak much English. They managed to communicate that they had walked some distance, and were shivering either from exhaustion or perhaps fear, as it was not cold.

With lots of calm persuasion and some positive signals the officers settled the girls into their vehicle, and after reporting into their duty officer took them to the Williamstown police station in Nelson Place — a 24/7 station with full search and rescue facilities, plus water police.

The duty officers had no success in conversation with the girls or any identification, so a callout was made to bring in an interpreter and to make the girls comfortable. They looked very young but opinion in the station favoured the opinion of their being illegal sex workers.

The first-choice interpreter invited to the police station was from Thailand and that at least was correct. She was able to converse with the women even though they were reluctant and very frightened. It became obvious that geographically they did not know where they were, and had most likely been held as prisoners. They had no identifying passports, name tags or wallets. They were young, tiny, and attractive, with both having a very demure and shy manner. The interpreter suggested a physical medical examination could be appropriate. That required a special authority.

Through slow and patient communications, it evolved that the girls been kept in isolation in a house close to the Science Works museum, just under the Bolte Bridge, and on occasions had been taken onto a luxury yacht/launch close to Williamstown Esplanade. They had been provided as 'companions' at all-male functions. Descriptions of locations were vague, but the essence of their descriptions resulted in a request for help from police head office, and that resulted in sending DCI Linda Alexander and Inspector Ian McDonald to Williamstown police station to decide if this was an event of merit requiring the resources of the newly created OCS (organised crime syndicates) division. Linda and Ian were allocated a spare office and any facilities needed. They tagged the case and the two young women 'The Milly and Mandy case'.

It was obvious from the limited information that the girls hesitantly and reluctantly presented that they were controlled and manipulated beyond any personal actions of their own and definitely had been held as prisoners. Linda decided that certainly there was a nasty criminal element involved.

The question she posed was, "how big and how organised?"

With perseverance and patience, plus the help of local ethnic specialists, it became evident that the women had been 'given' by their families in Thailand to criminals to pay off debts, and they had become locked into a life of controlled debauchery. They had been shipped anonymously to Melbourne under false passports to be used at the whim of local criminals. They were prisoners with other young women, controlled and kept by unknown masters.

From information elicited through the interpreter, it became apparent that the girls were kept in a locked back area of the Williamstown house that held up to six women at a time. The male guard who locked them in and brought their meals was described by them as, "big and ugly, tattoos on arms and body, long black hair in a ponytail, small moustache." He said very little but was hard to understand. Their English was limited, so they could not comment on his accent. The guard was unpleasant and they were scared of him. He stared at them and their bodies.

They were positive they had been taken on at least two occasions in a van a short distance to a boat — a launch or large yacht — where there was loud music, alcohol and drugs, but no food or drinks was allowed for them. They were pushed, prodded and sometimes punished. Tears welled in their eyes as they tried to tell of the experience. The events were mainly attended by men, but "a few female heads" were also there. The further the questioning progressed the more obvious it became that the two small women were being promoted as under-age children for lecherous old men to enjoy. The interpreters and the police officers were disgusted and angry.

Linda decided that the OCS should take over the inquiry with the help of officers from the Williamstown Station.

Additional officers could augment the inquiries as necessary. Linda knew the area well from previous experience.

The first action she asked for was for the local police to inquire about unusual people or activities around the waterfront, with emphasis on underage girls apparently being bullied. Nothing fitting that description had been reported but a matronly resident had reported an unusual "freakish-looking" hippie-type woman going into one of the main street shops. Her description was tall and skinny as a rake, spectacular boobs, dressed in a skimpy colourful lycra exercise outfit, with ugly dark-coloured tattoos up her neck to just under her chin, and the rest of her bare skin decorated with black tattoos featuring scrolls and words. Probably about thirty to forty years old. Rings in her lips, ears and nose, false dark eye lashes and black shiny lipstick, but most amazing of all she had a dog on a lead and was pushing a baby pram containing another dog under a blanket.

Best of all, when the elderly woman stared at the entourage, the tattooed one politely enquired in very correct English, "And what the fuck are you staring at?" No wonder the Williamstown resident remembered her.

Then the elderly woman added, "you know when facial cosmetics seem to have gone astray, and you get those fat lips — what I call a 'duck pout' mouth — that was her," when asked how on earth she could remember such detail.

The response left no doubt, "She was absolutely different from anything within my memory and a real shocker. Maybe she was from the sex industry?"

It did not take long for the police to establish where this unusual person was living. There had been no reports of suspicious behaviour but a watch was put out for her, with no apprehension instructions. The two officers enjoyed the low-key general community surveillance they had to do, and enjoyed the company of the many Williamstown seagulls circling their car making aggressive calls. Less than a day of watching had resulted in identification. "Easy peasy" was how the officer described the identification.

They had enjoyed the routine of coasting along, or sitting in one spot for hours on the neat and pretty esplanade with its attractive shops and restaurants, the fish and chips, the sporting facilities, the Navy ship and the major ship-building facilities. They simply followed the exotic-looking person home to establish the address.

It was easy then to find out who owned the large, two-storied wooden house two blocks back from the water's edge. Perhaps not surprisingly, the residence was owned by a city company that owned several other properties including two hotels, a city nightclub, a gymnasium, a fitness franchise, and some boating and marine interests. Among the various directors were a married couple who occasionally featured in media fashion columns. Their main residence was reputed to be in Sandringham where they were well known. Not considered pillars of society, and not 'flashy', but generous donors to local causes.

Linda set in motion the steps necessary to raid the Williamstown home, to arrest the suspects and to establish a connection to a launch or yacht that may have been used. All the necessary protocols were followed and even a call or two from Linda to a police friend in the AFP about likely hiding spots. He took delight in outlining the new technological aids available including X-rays, penetrating radar, metal detectors, high-end military technology and unravelling cryptology, and offered help if necessary. He alerted her to the levels of clever hiding places, such as false beams, hollow steering wheels, hydraulic doors, that had become more sophisticated. She thanked him generously.

The initial target was to establish the people smuggling and prostitution aspect of the inquiry, and the likely connection to drugs and money laundering.

13

The Raid

Linda, accompanied by her deputy Ian McDonald and one constable, led the raid. There was no aggressive resistance, except from a large, dark-skinned weight-lifter type guard who tried to stand in the way until the main object of the visit, the heavily tattooed woman, told him to back off.

The tattooed woman identified herself as Freda Zellerman, and was in possession of what appeared to be a legitimate UK passport and a current Australian visa. The bodyguard was Wirimu Williams. Both the apprehended people had tattoos covering most of their visible body parts, but when attempting to be civil to them with a query on the tattoos, the only response came from Freda Zellerman, who suggested she thought her coverage was decorative art rather than anything meaningful.

Documents readily available revealed the name and whereabouts of a luxury launch — currently moored at Southbank — where it was maintained and captained by a marine specialty company. Linda immediately took steps to search the vessel, named 'Pure Blue', but was not hopeful of a much from it as the company providing the maintenance was known to be professional, expensive and discreet.

The Williamstown address was much more fruitful. As expected, Freda Zellerman, being the extrovert she clearly was, admitted she was aware of the two missing women and now took the police to the room they had occupied, and introduced the officers to two additional sex workers housed in another part of the house. These young women were not so confused as the two girls picked up earlier, but nevertheless were otherwise also homeless and not 'free'.

It seemed that the two newly discovered girls were from the Philippines and spoke adequate, if hesitant, English. Referred to as Filipinas and actively used in the sex trade, they were little more than slaves who had been traded in the Philippines and their visas and passports retained by their 'masters'. This was clearly illegal as well as disgraceful and health officials were immediately called in. Freda was arrested and taken to the Williamstown police station, accompanied by records and documents that needed to be filtered through to establish ownership and responsibility for all or any of the activities uncovered.

The follow-through of the raid required data analysis and significant delving into names, addresses, dates and connections both locally and overseas. It provided an opportunity for Linda to take her first visit to the Auckland police and an opportunity for her deputy, Ian McDonald, to enact some leadership in his own right.

14
First New Zealand Trip

DI Alexander was picked up at Auckland International Airport by her equivalent officer in the NZ Police Force called Dennis Arkle, and given a genuinely friendly welcome. The plan was to share information and streamline communications to handicap organised crime. Introductions at Auckland head office were brief, and with good humour involving comments about sporting codes. From her childhood experience in South Africa, Linda could even exchange knowledgeable banter about Rugby Union — the New Zealand national game.

Being the major port for New Zealand, Auckland's shipping and airport areas presented opportunities for entry and exit for pretty much anyone and anything. Crime rates in drugs, prostitution, money laundering and physical violence were high.

The very large, modern, city-based casino provided facilities from excellent public entertainment to special accommodation for high rollers to maximise gambling opportunities. More mundane casino gambling games were also available at less salubrious premises in the more old-fashioned street known as 'K. Rd'. Full name Karangahape Road, it had been a major shopping destination in the past but now housed a much wider range of premises including homes for lower socio-economic dwellers.

Dennis explained to Linda that Auckland had a range of immigrants from the traditional areas of Europe (overtaking migrants mainly the UK from the old days) and more recently India and China, as well as smaller numbers from distressed war zones. Quite a mix. He wanted to emphasise there was really no specific racial discrimination as the original settlers, the Maori, were fully integrated. There was a different set of discussions involved about people from the Pacific Islands. Crime, as in most large cities, ranged over every possibility.

The subject of crime was the raison d'etre of the visit. Linda wanted to make contact with the owner of a company known to her from a previous case in Melbourne in which the company had been used to import product from Taiwan and India, and unknowingly had been used to hide and import serious drugs. A slightly social tangent but she thought it could be useful.

As anticipated, Joe McFadgen from Paramount Trading was delighted to take a call from her and invited her for a coffee the next day. He also said Dennis would be welcome to join them. A really co-operative attitude, as was typical.

Later in the day, after having visited the suburbs on the North Shore, and Mangere, Papakura, Panmure, and upmarket suburbs such as Remuera, Parnell and Epsom, Linda and

Dennis's discussion advanced to the use of drugs. Inspector Arkle went head first into outlining the real problem areas.

He said, "You know Linda, the drug problem and containing it is paramount in most of the western world. A country like New Zealand with its beautiful and open seaways, and like Australia with huge open beaches and land, is so easy to penetrate. The financial rewards are astronomical for the crooks."

He went to what was obviously his pet hate. Clearly it was cocaine, and the lesser evils of heroin, methamphetamine and cannabis. Away he went, even more angry about how little the growers — mainly in Columbia — received for the product from the shrub they had grown for centuries. His statistic was that sixty percent of cocaine was grown in Columbia and lesser amounts from Peru and Bolivia, but mainly controlled by one cartel.

Dennis went on, "It's disgraceful and so dishonest that the huge money is made through the many steps taken to convert the paste into powder that even then is further expanded or diluted for the market. Do you know all about the processing?"

Linda admitted she had some knowledge but Dennis was keen to go on. "It is the chemistry and processing that adds spectacularly to the product value and the profits rise by at least twenty times by simply moving the product, say, 5000 kilometres north to the USA. The problem is exacerbated by the monstrous profits made in each step of the distribution. The product generates huge cashflows for the participants who know how to bribe and protect their patches."

Even in little old NZ, he went on to add, the crooks were

awash with money and they were not shy to use it. Linda was quick to agree that the same circumstances applied in Melbourne and distribution of drugs was being made in all the known, and still unknown ways, both from the main bulk importers and the smaller crooks utilising 'mules'. High-profile sports stars and clubs, bikie gangs, gyms, massage and health clinics could all be involved. Linda, being a natural physical exerciser, frequented clubs and gyms and was obviously aware of body building and massage parlours, and studios. The money flowed like water at every level, and was packed into 'cash bricks' held together by rubber bands. They both agreed dishonest bureaucrats had to be part of the scenery.

Dennis was keen to show examples of brothels trading legally in K. Rd. and illegally in other areas. Auckland had identical problems with young people being involved in prostitution and being controlled by criminals who also controlled the supply of drugs and used violence to reinforce their control. With the city being a major port, restrictions were hard to enforce and the use of specialist high-speed courier launches for the pickup and distribution of products and people meant the organised crime syndicates were certainly well organised.

Linda could easily recognise the same modus operandi in action in NZ as back home. The visit was a real eye-opener for future joint operations and suggestions.

The coffee meeting with Joe McFadgen was pleasant. He, in his own way, emphasised the beauty of the many islands in the Hauraki Gulf, particularly Waiheke and Rangitoto Islands and how perfect they were for smuggling purposes! He also spoke about the large quantities of drugs being smuggled in as sea freight and hidden amongst legitimate products with their regulation permits and paperwork. He saw it as a difficult job for NZ Customs when criminals had so much money to use as a 'persuader' to so many.

Dennis agreed with these comments and the sentiment. Mention was made of the role played by the Royal New Zealand Air Force and its small but efficient part in the NZ Defence Forces. The RNZAF's primary roles were to provide surveillance, tactical air lifts, naval and fisheries support, using Boeing 757 and Hercules aircraft.

Back at police head office, discussions ranged over where the real 'heavies' were, and how far afield their tentacles may reach. There were, as in Australia, not openly acknowledged but were clearly known and identified specialists who could be available to carry out 'black ops'. There were, however, also some known fringe enforcers who had ambitions to mature into more serious undercover persuaders. They were on an unofficial list.

Linda asked, "Do you have a register or list of the known operators who clearly operate beyond the law with apparent immunity because they are so well set up and protected?" The answer was, "Yes, but they are known as the very deep and 'non-violent' manipulators."

The answer did not surprise her when Dennis went on, "Because of the amounts of cash involved there needs to be corrupt banks and bankers open to bribes, lawyers specialising in financial law, and corrupt officials in all areas. Yes, we are aware of some and we can monitor the lifestyles of the high fliers, but so many transactions are offshore and the money involved in tracking expenses, bribes, codes, encrypted messages, and violent enforcement makes it difficult to crack."

Linda could only nod and agree that it sounded similar to her knowledge of how so much of the serious crime was connected to crime syndicates, and even smaller groups such as motorbike gangs fitted in or fringed into the connection to big organised crime. More and more specialised expertise was needed to minimise the effects of criminality and more sophisticated and expensive equipment needed to penetrate these webs. It was apparent that there was a serious drug-use problem, with the attached level of criminal behaviour, in all levels of society. There were sophisticated types enjoying luxury lifestyles and socialising with pillars of society, living well-hidden drug-user lifestyles that were hard to isolate as they had friends and associates in key areas. These people had real clout.

Discussions ranged broadly and candidly about many subjects within organised crime.

15

Milly and Mandy

DI Linda Alexander finally headed home to Australia after four most enjoyable and informative days in Auckland. She needed another few days to summarise the visit and formulate recommendations to achieve benefits for both police forces. Much work had to be done and immediately exchanges of information commenced.

Linda returned to her role as Inspector in charge of her OCS division, which was currently investigating what appeared to be a nasty, large prostitution cohort that had expanded into under-age women and imprisoned illegal immigrants being held hostage in Williamstown. The more inquiries made, the bigger the ramifications became.

On her first day back after all the happy banter about visiting beautiful Auckland, Linda asked Ian McDonald to give her and the assembled team a summary of progress. He was pleased to do so and confidently gave the update.

"The two young girls from Thailand, aka Milly and Mandy,

are in custody and receiving medical care in preparation for return to their country," Ian advised. "The two women from the Philippines are being processed, as they are legitimately in Australia. The premises in Williamstown is probably ultimately owned by a Melbourne couple but well protected by shell and trust companies. The current user of the property appears to be a company that in turn has a legitimate business. The company has been investigated, as it has a luxury launch that was used for suspect social activities. The associates in these activities are of doubtful integrity and intent, and investigations are continuing. At least we have stopped their current activities."

Linda then asked, "And now what?"

Ian responded, "Freda Zellerman, aka the tattooed lady, is out on bail and has arranged private board, and Wirimu Williams has disappeared. Back to NZ?"

He went on to add, "The compiling of information on hand and arranging it into logical progression is straining our current resources. The biggest problem is to battle through the multiple levels of disguise or protection of the protagonists involved. We probably will need on-call legal expertise to cut through the rubbish to make sure we don't go off on tangents."

Linda's brief response was, "Understood!"

She straight away contacted her Superintendent to request clearance for legal help on-call, which was immediately approved with the assurance that additional administrative help would be also approved, when necessary. Without great emphasis, Linda then suggested to her team that a search for Wirimu Williams should be instigated. "Look at his flat, friends, and relations back in NZ," she added.

Ian commented that the search of ownerships of properties, boats and associations had highlighted the broad mix of people involved in organised syndicated crime. There was a range from real 'uglies' to the so-called 'beautiful people'. More than that, he said, they were international and very mobile.

Linda then outlined to her team what had been discussed in NZ, keeping the details brief but adding that future exchanges were envisaged. Similarities were commented on. It seemed probable that moving freight via sea and waterways added to the criminal options.

The team meeting discussed in detail the position of the 'Milly and Mandy' case. Jobs were allocated with emphasis on establishing the actual property owners, and separately, if the case, who the operators were. What functions could now be allocated to the individuals or companies connected to the illegally controlled women?

The owners/operators of the house in Williamstown needed closer dissection as it was obvious there was more than one level of control involved. Jobs were allocated, with instructions to report back to Linda.

The owner of the yacht had been established and activities contracted to it had been confirmed. Details of the duties and scheduled activities were required and full details of who had signed what contracts were needed. Jobs were again allocated, to report back to Ian McDonald.

Telephone tracing on every possible connection was to be urgently investigated.

A bit of a long shot instigated by Linda, and kept totally confidential from all except Ian McDonald, was to set in motion fact-finding about a particular couple — Anthony (Tony) Matheson and his wife, Janine. They owned and lived in a luxury home in Sandringham, and also owned the luxury launch identified and used in the shenanigans in Williamstown. The launch was not used by the Mathesons for personal use, it was leased out, and was actually moored over the winter at the Sandringham Yacht Club with another vessel owned by Janine Matheson that could only be described as a speed boat.

Tony Matheson was the owner of several franchises for imported luxury European cars and had a background in new and used car sales. He had advanced through property purchases and developments to be recognised as a community leader and influential political lobbyist. He was not part of the 'Old Boys' Melbourne clique, as he had not been educated in Victoria. He was not a member of any of the elite Melbourne men's clubs. He did, however, own the premises that housed the two best restaurants in the city.

The investigation into the owner/lessee of the large rambling house in Williamstown turned into a bit of a challenge. The talkative tattooed woman, Freda Zellerman, assured everyone that her boss was the actual owner of the establishment that operated the female escort business. She happily supplied the name and contact details for a Riccardo (Ricky) Russo. When contacted, Russo agreed he owned the business named Bella Companions, and his company leased the Williamstown property through a firm of upmarket city solicitors, and the company that owned the premises was registered as Perpetual Properties Pty Ltd. Further enquiries indicated that this was a shell company owned by a blind trust.

It was agreed that Linda and Ian McDonald would interview Ricky Russo. Over the telephone it was arranged to meet at the house in Williamstown the next day at 2pm.

Linda and Ian arrived promptly and parked outside the front door beside the only other car parked there, a shiny black Subaru. As they reached the front door, a man stepped forward in a friendly manner with his hand extended in greeting, saying, "Welcome! I'm Ricky Russo." The two police officers introduced themselves and as they moved into a neat, classically furnished foyer, Ricky took the opportunity to introduce a colleague, Deborah. She invited them to have coffee which the three agreed to, with thanks. While she went off to prepare the coffees, Ricky led them into an impressive large formal lounge. Pleasantries were exchanged until the coffee arrived and everyone was settled in.

The officers observed that Ricky Russo appeared to be in his late forties, with neatly cut black hair pulled back tightly into a short pony tail, an expansive very white smile, and a few grey hairs pushing up through his short shave. He wore what undoubtedly was an expensive watch under his neatly ironed black long-sleeved shirt, which was tucked into tight fashion slacks with the aid of a very smart black leather belt, all complimented by shiny black shoes. He was very smooth, and it appeared as if assistant Deborah had been fitted out from the same classy clothier.

Ricky had an easy, relaxed style and manner. In conversation he would drop in small interesting and humorous snippets that added to his charm.

"We could all adjourn to a local bar for a drink if we thought it would be more relaxing," he stated. "If you are not recording this conversation? Or do you perhaps think I should bring my lawyer along? Or is this just background information to the saga?" he continued, with a slight smile and a upwards pucker of his lips.

Linda volunteered, "Well, perhaps better words would be: it's preliminary!"

Ricky arrogantly replied, "Why?"

Inspector Ian McDonald had been sitting quietly in a comfortable lounge chair enjoying his coffee. He leaned forward, flexing large and strong arms that emphasised his well-muscled exterior, and in the quietest, but threatening, voice said, "I'll tell you why. We don't like crooks like you abducting and using under-age women for sex and in S&M activities specialising in bondage etc." Ricky was clearly a little taken aback, but Deborah was very rattled.

Ricky then leapt to his feet protesting loudly, "I've not done any of those things! You are trying to fit me up!"

Calmly Linda added, "So tell us all about yourself and how you fit into this melting pot that we have discovered. Be sure to include your connection with the yacht's activities. Start with were you come from."

Russo now realised he could be in trouble, so he decided to cooperate. First though, he stressed that Deborah was an innocent inclusion as she had been only recently employed, and only as 'eye-candy'. He was born and bred in Sydney where he had graduated through his teens stealing cars or trail bikes, and that also included stealing keys from homes, joyriding the vehicles until they ran out of fuel or crashed and were written off; making deliveries of drugs on behalf of 'heavies' and receiving cash in return; then helping out in night clubs — straight from juvenile crime to assistant to a club owner, who saw potential in him for his sense of style, good looks and agile mind. He was aware of some of the nefarious activities in the club scene, and had witnessed police raids and community efforts to try to sterilise the range of behaviour and prostitution that was associated with it.

Ricky had adapted well to the club scene, and worked his way up as opportunities presented themselves. He commented that as in all professions, ambition and ego also played a part. He had progressed to a larger club where he was involved when the police made a major raid and he was included in a minor way as an associate. He stressed his conviction was minimal but the club did run some very dodgy activities. With the help of a benefactor, he was encouraged to move to Melbourne.

Over several years, with connections through his uncle, a wealthy retired magistrate previously involved in the gay nightclub scene, Ricky became involved in the food and beverage business, providing services to large events such as major sporting occasions, race meetings, car racing, indoor and outdoor events. It included the associated supports such as marquees, security and parking. A comprehensive package of utilities to manage. Linda and Ian were impressed.

Ricky went on to tell how he became involved in the Williamstown residence. His retired uncle, Paul Wheeler, rented a house which was tidy and anonymous to entertain some of his gay friends, and to also use at times to impress more important straight people and companies when expanding his business portfolio. Ricky was involved in providing the supports to these events of his uncle's. Somewhere along the way, he had met Freda Zellerman and become entangled in her web of charm and energy. This new person in his life coincided with the declining interest that had been associated with his Uncle Paul, so there was time to explore new ideas.

Linda and Ian, looking closely at Russo, noticed he seemed to be enjoying immensely the telling of all this, his personal story. He began to confidently elaborate on some of his involvements and how clever he was, much of which was detail about various call girls and organising orgies.

Ian stepped in and cut him back to reality by insisting that his best chance for leniency was telling the truth about his involvement in the Milly-Mandy affair and all the repercussions, including drug supply and use on the yacht.

Ricky's smooth and confident demeanour gradually disappeared as Linda now explained, "Your current low level of illegal involvement that we know of can only get more serious as our investigations widen."

The officers noticed a pulse beating by his eye that his finger involuntarily moved to touch. A tiny twitch.

Linda, trying to be helpful, suggested, "We want lists of

the guests who attended the party on the yacht Pure Blue, and the names of all the staff who worked at the Williamstown residence. Details of the leasing of the yacht, and arrangements with all suppliers and entertainers for events. Of course, we will need to see financial results for Bella Companions and the role that Freda Zellerman plays and what she controls," she added. "That will do to start with, but our expectations of your full cooperation are much greater."

Russo was surprised, and even Inspector McDonald was impressed by the request.

Ricky Russo was now fidgety, and the little flicker by his eye became more pronounced. He pleaded, "You know I can't possibly supply that information! Some of it I don't have and the rest would see me eliminated in the ugliest possible way. These are powerful and vicious people!"

16
Ownership and Lawyers

Linda replied to Ricky, "Let's make the first bit easy for you; tell us all about Freda Zellerman."

Russo was much more at ease on the description of her role. She was the 'madam', he explained, who controlled all the call girls and the prostitution organisation overall. Freda did not report to him in the business, but they were sexual partners. Together they planned and delivered all the events. She could, and did, provide high-end escorts for individual clients, those with special requests at prices well in excess of normal sexual favours. Prices could be for an entire evening, or just short visits, and were graduated depending on the various services rendered and even the size of the budget.

Ricky was not quite sure when and where Freda had emerged from to end up managing the call girls. He assured the officers that she alone procured or introduced the women from overseas origins, and had never disclosed to him the source or line of supply they came from.

The officers looked at each other — could that really be accepted? Ricky emphasised that Freda definitely controlled their health, welfare and behaviour. He claimed to be in charge but he was adamant that Freda Zellerman had a different line of communication and responsibility within the organisation.

The routine day-to-day control of Bella Companions was administered by Ricky Russo under instruction from the company solicitor. The dates, size, type, style, venue and likely number of attendees were texted to him well in advance of the proposed dates. His responsibilities included pulling together support material and trustworthy staff, chauffeurs and cars, food and beverages, boats, music, and even 'rent a crowd' if deemed to be appropriate. The company storage facilities in Kororoit Creek Road, Altona, was where they housed equipment such as tables and chairs, video and musical equipment. There were also well-hidden supplies of alcohol and other stimulants there. Ricky described it as an efficient and secure set-up.

He went on to admit that drugs, mainly ice, were a usual commodity at these events, but they were always sourced from a local known dealer, i.e. not from a big crime syndicate. More elaborate drugs such as cocaine and others were sometimes requested. Ricky admitted he dabbled in the jazz scene and regularly attended gigs in clubs in the city and suburbs. In answer to a question, he replied that he personally had no involvement with or interest in underage females.

The solicitor from whom he received information had always stressed that he was acting on behalf of an anonymous third party. Ricky neither handled payments to any creditors nor collected any debts. Because of his background and the very generous remuneration he was paid, he had never thought to question the system, though he did wonder occasionally who the real boss was and had heard it speculated by some that he was a polo-playing, playboy pillar of society based in Adelaide. However, it was just a rumour.

Asked about how he got access to the yacht and how he coordinated moorings, fuelling, and anchoring, Ricky acknowledged that that was all arranged through the solicitor, or another company employee.

Back in the office, Linda and Ian realised that a large amount of research was needed, much of it routine and much of it requiring deep digging into ownerships. A full history of Ricky Russo and the same on Freda Zellerman and all known associates of both of them would be required, plus full details of owners, lessees, companies, trustees, and an inspection of the storage property in Altona; motor vehicles registered to company's family or friends; details of all known communications equipment, and a dig for encryption systems. They would need to check the firm of solicitors that apparently acted as a major communicator, and names of those liaising with Russo, Zellerman and the uncle, Paul Wheeler.

Linda asked for particular focus to be put on Freda Zellerman as she was thought to be a serious career criminal with a track record back in the UK and most probably also in Ireland.

Linda went on, "Who owns the trading names and controls the Pure Blue yacht and Bella Companions? Look for some strange or 'outside' inclusion."

Perseverance was the word used often now to the police team, who in turn suggested more help or staff was needed. It was obvious that somewhere deep inside all these activities people smuggling was taking place.

That prompted Linda to see if she could recruit her friend and associate Beth Jenkins. By good luck, she was informed she could have the Leading Senior Constable for three months as she was available for that short period as her new promotion/position was not available until then. Great news, and upon Beth's arrival, many files were assembled into her office space to keep her very busy. Linda and Ian planned an explorative interview with Tony Matheson in Sandringham, and also booked another quick trip for Linda to NZ.

Amid the urgent concentration on suspects and inquiries, the usual invitations to senior police officers flooded in. Superintendent Ron Brunton was a popular invitee to sports events as he had been a star footballer in his youth and was known to follow all codes. He received an invitation to the AFL season highlight, a Saturday game between traditional rivals Collingwood and Carlton. The invitation for two came through a Reg McGuiness as a public relations gesture, which McGuiness excelled at. The police force was equally keen to have good exposure at a neutral venue so Superintendent Brunton invited Linda to accompany him to the match. As a keen sportsperson, she was delighted to accept.

On arrival at the Melbourne Cricket Ground, known around the world as the MCG, they were welcomed by McGuiness and taken to an elite members-only viewing box and offered a variety of canapes, savouries and other nibbles, and an array of drinks.

Neither officer was naïve enough to be seen or photographed with anything other than water in hand but they were happy to be introduced to other members enjoying the pre-game socialising, and the anticipated excitement of the game.

Reg McGuiness in his usual gregarious manner took them around to meet other attendees, there being quite a few who Ron Burton knew. One was introduced as John Silverman, who was Reg McGuiness's deputy manager in his public relations company. Later, in a quiet private corner, Linda asked if the Superintendent had ever met Silverman before, to which he responded, "No, why do you ask?"

Linda replied, "He didn't seem like the usual marketing type to me; he didn't look me in the eye at all, and the hairs on the back of my neck twitched."

"Being intuitive?" he quizzed her, as they moved on to enjoy the afternoon.

17

Ricky and Freda

Anthony (aka Tony) Matheson and his wife Janine were surprised at the police request to meet, but graciously agreed for Linda and Ian to go to their home in Sandringham for a morning meeting. Linda, in neat plain clothes, and Ian in full police uniform arrived on time in their clearly marked police vehicle. They were greeted a little warily at the front door of the substantial and immaculately attractive residence slightly up the hill from the shops and railway station.

Almost together the couple said, "Welcome to our home. Please come in."

The officers introduced themselves formally, admiring the decor as they walked across to a formal lounge, then outside to a patio area where orders for coffee or tea were taken.

As soon as the refreshments arrived and they were all settled, Janine directly asked, "Well what's this all about then, officers?"

Linda thanked them for being available and outlined the

reasons. Their interests were in the home in Dalton Street, Williamstown, which was apparently owned by a company that Tony Matheson was a director of, and also the ownership of the luxury yacht Pure Blue, managed by some sports personnel using the name Agile Athletes, all of which were used by a company called Bella Companions.

The single word response from Tony was, "Fascinating!" Ian McDonald added that the yacht was domiciled in the off-season right here at the Sandringham Yacht Club.

Janine Matheson, confident and full of charm, said, "Well, I have never heard of them and I don't even know where Dalton Street, Williamstown, is."

To be helpful, Linda added, "We think Mr Matheson may have a vested interest in both properties and our interest is because they are involved in international organised crime, which we are investigating."

It now seemed less fascinating to both Mr and Mrs Matheson. Tony was much more attentive and suggested that the main enquiry, with his help, could be directed to his solicitor who handled all his personal financial affairs and most of his company connections. He positively asserted that he had no direct connection to either of the properties alluded to. Tony did go on to confirm he was a member of various clubs — the Sandringham Yacht Club, Sandringham Dragons Football Club, the Northern Men's Club, where his solicitor Samuel Hoggard was a fellow member, and of the Brighton Rotary Club — and a generous philanthropic donor. His main source of income was from company board directorships and investment properties.

He suggested that future questions should be directed through solicitor Sam Hoggard.

Politely the officers were sent on their way, thus providing another line of inquiry for Beth Jenkins and the back-office team to home in on. They were not a bit sure whether they had in any way rattled his cage, or merely been another subject for them to discuss with friends. It seemed to Linda and Ian that on the surface the Mathesons were the epitome of clean.

Back in the station, Linda repeated her previous emphasis to the team to dig deep and follow the smallest lead to connect to any already identified personnel, to users or suppliers of illegal products or services. A big range, and to include any possible and willing recipients of bribes in known areas such as customs and border control, stating, "they do exist."

Nil results so far in the search for Wiremu Williams.

18
Second NZ Trip

Linda's second visit to NZ was made to exchange information, including about connections to the Pacific Islands. There seemed to be a disproportionate number of NZ Islanders in trouble in the courts in Australia.

Linda's counterpart Dennis Arkle wanted to define for her more clearly 'who was who' amongst the Islanders. He directed Linda to an office containing a large whiteboard and proceeded to give her a quick lesson about the South Pacific. He explained, in order of size, that the totally independent countries were Fiji, Tonga, Vanuatu, Samoa and Tahiti. NZ dependencies were the Cook Islands and Tokelau. Australian dependencies were Christmas Island, Cocos Islands and Norfolk Island. Then there were other smaller islands.

Most of the people of the various dependencies were lumped together under the description of 'Islanders' and were able to enter NZ remarkably easily, and therefore had easy access to Australia. In many cases they appeared no different from NZ Maori. They followed and played similar sports and integrated comfortably unless they broke the law. Dennis reiterated that there was a natural competitive inclination between New Zealanders and Australians and NZ still had a feeling of inferiority about Australia being 'big brother'. The average Kiwi (New Zealander) was fiercely independent.

Drugs use unfortunately seemed to be of similar pro rata proportions, and as many NZ sports relied on physical excellence, the use of body building steroids was in the mix. Alcoholic stimulants of all types were readily available legally, and smuggled in as well. Inspector Arkle made the point that illegal products were being exchanged both ways between Australia and NZ as illicit products were moved by enterprising criminals on both sides of the Tasman Sea. Products such as cocaine, diazepam, methamphetamines, and precursor chemicals could be imported in small quantities and still be very valuable. The coastlines of both countries were remote and ideal for droppages offshore, to be picked up later by small speed boats.

On a more pleasant basis, Dennis took Linda to visit the naval base at Devonport and the air force base at Hobsonville, both close to the Auckland CBD, to see the surveillance equipment used to safeguard the shores. He also accompanied her to Tauranga in the Bay of Plenty to see the second-biggest overseas port from which woodchips were exported in bulk carriers. Ideal vessels in which to hide illegal imports, thought Linda.

All these localities were low-population spots and difficult to control. The big question for all police forces was to identify the professional organised criminal elements who were usually deeply hidden but nevertheless controlling actions by remote control. There were the middle activators, and then down the line multiple layers of distributors and users. Inspector Arkle confessed he was not sure that his team had it all fully identified and under control, nor was he sure about how each criminal section was scoring or benefiting from the drug scene.

Linda admitted that there was no clarity on the same subject in Australia. They had serious long chats about where the majority of drug imports were perhaps originating from, i.e., which country or even which drug lord's establishment? Perhaps constantly changing?

The comfortable atmosphere between the two police officers was evolving, as they were both career people, knew how cops thought, and respected each other's opinions. They even discussed racial and sexual discrimination and agreed it existed but was quite different in both countries. The 'Islanders' were blamed for many things unfairly in NZ.

Enquiries about Wiremu William's family connections were useful. He came from a large family in Mangere, south of Auckland, and had no track record with police before he left for Australia three years before. His older brother Gordon lived in Otahuhu, also south of Auckland, where he was a senior member of a large motorbike gang. When Wiremu first moved to Australia, he lived in Sydney where he, too, was briefly in a motorbike gang, before moving on to Melbourne. All useful information for Linda, as supplied by Dennis Arkle.

Back in Auckland, Dennis invited Linda to have a meal with him and his wife, Amanda, at the SkyCity Auckland Casino complex. A treat for her, but also acknowledgement of the comfortable relationship being built up between the two colleagues. A nice gesture to include his wife, and humanise the hard work being put in. Amanda and Dennis were great company and immediately the women relaxed together. They all first viewed parts of the complex. Two casinos, multiple restaurants and bars, a hotel and the 328-metre-high Sky Tower, a tourist attraction in itself. Dennis disclosed that there were over 2000 gaming machines and 150 table games. A real 'den of iniquity' that was not lost on the visiting police officer. The informative evening was topped off by a relaxed dinner and a glass of wine that helped cement the free flow of honest communications for the future between two senior and serious law enforcers, and with Linda hearing all about the Arkle family as well.

Next morning, before Linda was scheduled to fly back to Australia, Inspector Arkle convened a meeting his senior staff to discuss at length the possibilities and probabilities of international crime syndicates having infiltrated the local crime scene in NZ. It was unanimously agreed that there was a high level of opportunity and therefore probability of illegal transactions occurring both ways across the Tasman. The Army, Navy and Air Force, and airlines such as Air NZ, Virgin and Qantas all conducted daily air transactions and freight movements, as did the major freight-moving companies. There were both large and small ships. Many companies were involved, such as Hills Industries, Linfox, Toll group, Coles, Woolworths, general fruit and vegetable growers, Paramount Trading, DHL, Specsavers, car and truck importers, large and small manufacturers moving stock inter- company or as a single sale; all moving products on a regular basis through the ports and airports. They all employed staff, some of whom could be tempted to look the other way for a bribe. Cruise ships including passengers and staff were also regular possibilities for illegal activities.

Government officials, Customs officers and wharf employees all had opportunities to participate. Added to those were the professional smugglers, the sailors, and one-off opportunists - who could include sporting stars and icons – and there were also the rogue skilled but criminally inclined associates of motor bike groups. A big number to realise the potential size and value of smuggled goods. The list was huge and rewards enormous, even by moving small quantities of products, such as drugs.

The group discussed human trafficking, as Linda volunteered information about the Australian case of 'Milly and Mandy'. Human trafficking in NZ was identified as a crime, and NZ participated in the Asia Pacific region under a role in the so-called 'Bali Process'. The NZ Police did not identify such trafficking as a large problem but had had instances of victims from India and Thailand. They watched in particular for underage females from the Pacific Islands being used as sex slaves. There seemed to be no anxiety about the exchange of information between forces.

Dennis in a friendly voice said specifically to Linda, "We need to get a big map for you to look at our coastline. Particularly the west coast facing Australia. From Kawhia to Raglan, to Dannevirke and the Hokianga Harbour, Rawene, and the Ninety-mile Beach. All lightly populated with easy beach access. A smugglers paradise!" From her small experience of NZ, Linda in reply quipped, "Think I should come and live here!" That got a laugh and applause from the group.

The size of the challenge was appreciated from both sides of the Tasman and all the difficulties had already been acknowledged. The Inspectors openly discussed the bigger problem relating to overseas organised crime syndicates and their ability to infiltrate the local, more personalised groups. This could be done without the locals even realising the penetration.

As Linda pointed out, the prime movers/major players and even the second tier down were not easily identified as participants or criminals ('crooks' in local police lingo). She admitted, "In Melbourne alone, we have two or three prime suspects as to who the 'Mr Big' might be, but haven't yet nailed it. Do you have such candidates in Auckland?"

The answer from Dennis, accompanied by head nodding, was, "Of course!"

It was agreed that value was arising from the police interchange and would be progressed. Linda returned to Melbourne and reported to her boss.

19
Digging for Details

Linda and Beth met for an update.

Beth reported that the police force team data mining or 'digging' was progressing well and information about Freda Zellerman, in particular, was growing. She was an experienced and senior member of an offshore syndicate. Beth Jenkins was like a terrier as she chased down every lead. It turned out that Ms Zellerman was in fact a Mrs Zellerman, previously Miss Holloway from Soho, London, were she had a track record with police and a criminal record. She had mainly been involved in prostitution offences, both as an organiser and a participant. Before departing from London, Freda was known to be associated with some very heavy eastern European groups, known to be extremely physical to be persuasive. Also, there was an as yet to be confirmed lead to a relative from Northern Ireland, but no record or details yet of Mr Zellerman.

Freda had arrived in Australia with legitimate documentation two years previously and had no adverse reports to date. Her current address was an apartment in Russell Street, in the central Melbourne CBD, not far from the big RMIT University at the La Trobe Street end. It seemed that she worked for Ricky Russo and Bella Companions, but further enquiries revealed it was probable that Ricky Russo actually reported to Freda Zellerman, and they may well be casual sexual partners.

Linda observed, "An interesting mix that could suggest Freda Zellerman could be the experienced operator in human trafficking? Is Russo a willing apprentice?"

Beth then reported the team were making excellent progress, and after presenting a summary she asked Linda if they could have a coffee or drink after work, as she had some points, she would like further guidance on.

Linda was quick to agree, "That would be great Beth, because I hope you can stay with the team for as long as possible, and it would be good for a wider update and for me to tell you about Inspector Dennis Arkle in Auckland."

So that was what they did. Linda was keen to talk about how impressed she was with how Dennis Arkle was successfully running his police life as a married family man, and thought Beth Jenkins could do the same. Beth had previously confessed to Linda that her new promotion may stress her marriage.

The discussion continued with Beth asking Linda, "Do you really think I can handle the role of Sergeant in a station where I will need to make some decisions on my own?"

Linda energetically assured her, "No problem at all, you are an experienced officer that the police force has invested a lot of time and money in, and I personally think you have all the qualifications necessary to 'slay' the job!" They grinned and hugged each other, and as on previous occasions knew they would be life-long friends.

Linda asked, "OK, then how much longer do I have your dedicated support on this project?" Beth admitted that it was probably only two more months at the most, so they had better get on with it and they could discuss later what additional help would be needed. Linda said she would not visit NZ again until further progress was made.

20

Data Mining for Facts

The constant reassessing of the current level of established facts highlighted the need to further look at Ricky Russo, the missing Wiremu Williams, and Paul Wheeler (Ricky's uncle), being a supplier of drugs. The inquiries were being sent out far and wide, and particularly, but more discreetly - about Tony Matheson.

The detail that had been compiled so far on Ricky Russo was interesting as he was known to frequent and in fact also work at several sex shops specialising in high-end sex aids. These outlets were in a rough triangle of Russell Street, Exhibition Street and Mackenzie Street, in the northern Melbourne CBD. There were also two other premises in Russell Street; one called Club X, and the other 'FlingTasia', that were owned by or leased to the same operator, as yet unknown. Ricardo (aka Ricky) Russo was clearly an integral part of whichever outfit was running the visible part of the business. Enquiries led back to the elusive solicitor Samuel Hoggard at the firm of Randle and Randle, lawyers, in Collins Street, Melbourne.

Ricky's mysterious uncle Paul Wheeler was not so difficult to ferret out. He was now an elderly openly practising homosexual, who had been prosecuted many years previously for obscene behaviour when the laws were more uncompromising. As a young man he had inherited a large amount of money that had made him independent and less tolerant of what he perceived as idiots. He had a wide range of friends, male and female, and was respected as a polished member of Melbourne society, and influential within the local gay community. Paul lived in a substantial and stylish home in Winmalee Road, Balwyn, an outer upmarket Melbourne suburb, where he sometimes he held wonderful fancy-dress parties to which many important Melburnians were invited. On various occasions Paul had used the legal services of Randle and Randle, but there were no records of any property ownership. Police reports suggested he was a well-groomed, flamboyant and colourful personality, who had a polished and opaque demeanour when being interviewed or interrogated.

Added to this workload were two new cases for the OCS to concentrate on. One case involved a small and enterprising group of retired star rugby league players who jointly owned two Cessna aircraft and had several members with licences to fly. The aircraft had the range to fly over 400 kilometres and the flexibility to fly in and out of smaller airports. Drugs, alcohol and sex workers were their passengers, and there was a loose connection to a major motorcycle gang.

The second additional case involved the activities of a well-established eastern European - group based in the Brunswick area. They were well known and identified, but had now begun to recruit, encourage, and pay for blatant burglaries by underage new immigrants from Africa. The new members were being sent on missions to target specific products, such as jewellery, and specifically diamonds.

The most significant addition to the division's case load was the discovery of a body washed up on a beach not far from Warrnambool, in south-west Victoria. The body was very damaged, but the most significant factor was that both hands and ankles were securely tied together. Time and examination established that it was the body of the missing Wiremu Williams. It also established that those involved in his demise were vicious, as Williams had been tortured and his body disposed of well out to sea. Speculation received from police informers was that Williams had been murdered by a 'master' contract killer, but it was hoped 'someone will talk and give us a name'. Would forensics reveal clues?

The increasing workload and the impending departure of friend Beth Jenkins prompted Linda to ask her boss to consider finding a new recruit for the OCS. She knew this would take time but hoped it would be filled within the two months before Beth took up her new position. Her boss, Superintendent Ron Brunton, was sympathetic to the request but not optimistic. A few weeks later he called Linda into his office and, looking pleased with himself, advised her that a very smart constable was available. Her name was Helen Murphy, a one-stripe constable with ambition to specialise as a detective.

The name immediately rang a bell with Linda, and then she recalled to Ron Brunton that Murphy was a mature recruit who apparently looked a little like her and had been bold enough, or silly enough, to express admiration for Linda. Ron had known Linda for many years and was careful to emphasise that Murphy had done well in her Academy training and was an intelligent and enthusiastic officer.

Linda mentioned she had also heard Helen could be belligerent with those she thought to be inferior. Ron said he understood she was perceived as 'pushy' but felt sure Linda could maximise the good and minimise the bad traits. There would be a gap of a month before the change would take place.

Naturally, Linda told Beth who her replacement would be and also went on to ask her to make some discreet enquiries about the new recruit — "As a friend, Beth? Perhaps sleuth around for me, absolutely confidentially! And we can talk about your findings over a glass of red, next Thursday at the Aster?"

Beth was also investigating solicitor Samuel Hoggard who seemed to be 'the Man' from whom, or to whom, Ricky Russo and/or Freda Zellerman made most reference. The firm he was associated with now was established to be Randle and Randle, Lawyers, a well-known firm who now apparently had no one called Randle engaged in company activities. The partners listed, totalling eight, included no-one called Samuel Hoggard. One of the senior partners had attended Xavier College and Melbourne University at the same time as Tony Matheson, as had the high-profile radio and TV personality Reggie McGuinness, and were all still in touch with each other.

They, like hundreds of other fanatical AFL team supporters, were long-term financial members of their side the Richmond Tigers. They and their partners socialised together regularly.

Reggie came from a wealthy family in the top-flight Melbourne suburb of Armadale, and had drifted through Xavier College using his friendly personality into a low-key degree in arts, from where he moved straight into a large advertising agency.

Details of the structure of Randle and Randle, Lawyers, were not hard to discover; it appeared to be structured in a regular way, in that new partners were invited in and expected to contribute financially to the company, and then to reap the rewards in the future accordingly. The senior partner was a well-known and respected QC of the highest integrity. No scandal or skeletons were known or came to light with investigations. He was also a known and visible fan of the Richmond Tigers. Randle and Randle undoubtedly conducted normal regular business both interstate and internationally, as it was a very substantial practice.

Samuel Hoggard seemed a much more likely candidate to be fringing close to the less respectable. Police digging and investigations were to be continued.

21

Reassessing Evidence

Beth Jenkins was, with the help of some of her internal police friends and contacts, able to probe into the background of Helen Murphy. Her progress through the Police Academy to Senior Constable had caused some comment along the way.

The consensus definition of Helen, from contacts who insisted on being anonymous, was that she was narcissistic. On asking for elaboration of their understanding of the word, many descriptions were volunteered.

Some commented that it was a personality disorder mainly found in men. Helen had an almost total lack of genuine empathy. More pertinent were comments about arrogant thinking and self-importance. It was reported back that Helen was aware of her own need for admiration, and often countered it with a sly sense of humour.

Genuine delegation was not in her vocabulary. One of Beth's informants volunteered the theory that Helen had had a terrible childhood. Another said simply that Helen was manipulative.

A final opinion was that what she had was probably incurable.

These opinions were always accompanied by cautious qualification. Most contacts agreed they did not really know much about narcissistic personalities. They usually added, "She is very smart, you know," and added with a nod and wink, that her background must have been whitewashed, and she had support from higher up.

Unsubstantiated rumour has an amazing way of getting around and no one suggested that treatment could help, and that diagnosis needed medical input. Almost certainly the psychological support and counselling Helen had had as a child had made her aware of her strengths and weaknesses. She clearly had to apply concentration to maintain her equilibrium, and to separate her natural instinct from a giveaway reaction.

Beth commented to Linda that a soft friendly recommendation that did not invite a hostile response or reaction perhaps needed to be recognised by her. A "let it go through to the keeper" comment. Always be looking for harmony.

Soon after her posting to the OCS division and while still doing her general training and gaining exposure to the cases being prosecuted, Helen — accompanied by the officer doing the introductions — came into the cafeteria for a coffee break, where Linda, Beth and Ian McDonald were having a friendly and loud discussion on the merits of holidaying in Bali. They joined the group.

Beth was expounding her opinion about the warm climate and lifestyles in the tropics, "You know we should all aspire to go and live there — a lovely gentle lifestyle, contributing to a fair community." Ian and Linda added to the discussion, as they thought it sounded great but perhaps exaggerated.

Linda said, "Gee, that's an interesting opinion, what do you think, Constable Murphy?" seeking to include Helen.

Without hesitation Helen responded, "That's total rubbish. I have experienced that, and those people, and it's a total waste of time!" That quickly threw cold water on the conversation and the occasion, and gave Linda, Ian, and Beth a subject for future discussion. There was no attempt to minimise the effect with humour or even a softening of the words. Helen on first meeting did seem to be opinionated, sharp-tongued and even aggressive; not appreciative of an early opportunity to join the 'team' or even just initially sit quietly and observe the other members' dynamics.

The coffee break finished, and as Linda strolled back to her office, Beth and her assistant both offered opinions that so far, they had not heard Helen ever make a positive comment along the lines of, "You know that's a great idea, or a big improvement!"

22

Helen Murphy

Back in the team meeting room, Linda wanted to explore whether in the trafficking case of Milly and Mandy, there was any involvement of motorcycle gangs; any mild or heavy involvement, such as money laundering of cash through casino activities. The automatic next step from that possibility was to focus on the role played by the solicitor Samuel Hoggard who worked from within the framework of the Randle and Randle legal practice. The prime reason for this was that Hoggard seemed to be the 'common-connecting' name referred to by the two prime suspects in the human trafficking exposed in Williamstown.

An appointment was made for DI Linda Alexander and Sergeant Beth Jenkins to meet Sam Hoggard in his city office. Randle and Randle, Lawyers, occupied almost half of the twentieth floor of a large multi-storey building in the 'Paris end' of Collins Street, east Melbourne CBD.

Linda was dressed seriously in a modest fashion, suiting

her status, and Beth was in full police uniform, including cap. Stepping from the lift straight into the large foyer, they were greeted by a receptionist who took their tea or coffee orders. They were then escorted to a boardroom where Sam Hoggard greeted and welcomed them as their drinks arrived.

Hoggard was well groomed, around forty to forty-five years of age and very confident. A slight accent indicated he was originally from the UK. After the pleasantries, it was clear he understood that they were seeking information about ownership of a number of properties, and his position relative to events that evolved from the two illegal underage immigrants who had been housed in Williamstown.

He indicated he was aware of the situation and asked, "What is it you need to know?" All in a most charming manner. Linda was leading the conversation, and in an effort to focus his attention she cut straight to the personal questions.

She offered, "Thanks for seeing us so readily; we have ascertained you are not a partner here in this firm, but clearly you are an attorney who has been admitted to the bar, so a little of your background would be appreciated, and to whom you report could be helpful."

Not a bit perturbed by her directness, he said that he was forty-two years of age, educated in the UK, completed law at University in London, had migrated to Melbourne ten years ago as a law graduate, and was fortunate to have a cousin — a partner in Randle and Randle — who had aided him in being admitted into the firm as an attorney. All delivered very succinctly.

Both Linda and Beth expressed genuine thanks as they took notes. They went on to ask, "Now we require information about Freda Zellerman and Ricky Russo, who seem to be saying that they have communications with you for guidance and instructions."

That created a temporary stop in the free-flowing conversation so Linda added, "And what also can you tell us about another character, Paul Wheeler, and the ownership of properties in Williamstown under the name of Perpetual Properties, plus a warehouse in Kororoit Road, Altona, and companies trading as Bella Companions, Agile Athletes, and a motor yacht called Pure Blue?"

Beth added helpfully, "That should be enough to start with."

Sam Hoggard said, "No knowledge of Kororoit Road. Naturally officers, I take these questions on notice, and receive them as general and non-aggressive enquiries."

Linda responded in a soft, low voice: "We are a recently formed specialty police unit concentrating on organised crime syndicates, known as the OCS team, so we do have extra powers and authority to carry out confidential enquiries. High on our priority list is to investigate money laundering, importation and distribution of illegal drugs, human trafficking, prostitution, and violence."

After a pause, and with added emphasis in her voice, Linda carried on: "Now, to illustrate our current position of knowledge, I'll outline our informal information gathered about Freda Zellerman. Her mother was only sixteen when Freda was born in Ireland, and she was put into an orphanage. Her family did not want to know her but her mother was reluctant to sign adoption papers. She was shuffled from foster home to foster home. She did her share of stealing — school books, pencils — random stuff. She was counselled but she didn't care. She was a difficult child, but what would one expect?

"As we understand it, her major piece of 'luck' was to form a close relationship with another teenager of similar background and they stayed friends together through hardships and occasional attention from the Garda, and then they travelled to London for casual work. Many years and a wide range of experiences later, she and her then boyfriend entered the world of crime. For someone so uneducated she was a quick learner, and moved up the ladder to more sophisticated crimes, taking on the lessons learned from within her new crime family. Freda's mindset enabled her to embrace the physical and violent behaviour so often associated with prostitution. Probably as a form of protection, she married early after her arrival in London to a middle-aged gang leader. That allowed her some scope to reinvent her looks and persona."

There was a small break while Linda looked for any reaction from Hoggard before continuing. "The case of Mr Ricky Russo is different; he is a local lightweight who is a 'would be if he could be'. He in fact is a sleaze, working in the sex industry, from whom we expect to extract heaps of information."

It was not missed by the police officers that Hoggard had trouble hiding a smirk on his face.

To finish the meeting with Samuel Hoggard, Beth now kicked in with her contribution: "I'm one of the expert team researching the money laundering and human trafficking that seems to be associated with these young girls in Williamstown. We are particularly interested in anonymous shell companies, secret bank accounts, and methods of cleansing dirty money."

Almost as an afterthought she added, "We believe huge amounts of Russian money are being directed and filtered through to Australia from London, and thus we are very interested in your Ms Zellerman."

That provoked a reaction from Hoggard. "What's this all about? Why are you pressuring me?"

Linda took over in a more belligerent fashion. "I'm glad you asked that, and here is a set of reasons. You are clearly involved in activities using the contributions of two known felons, namely Freda Zellerman and Ricky Russo. They are involved in trafficking and money laundering. We are well aware of shonky banks in Samoa, the Cayman Islands, Guernsey etc. that can be used. We are connecting the purchase of assets such as properties, shares, buildings and companies in Melbourne using the established 'mirror system' to move funds from dirty money to clean. The casino is an obvious pathway, and the use of encrypted messages is no longer a sure method to escape detection. You should be aware that the Australian Federal Police in La Trobe Street are also very interested."

Complete silence engulfed the room as Hoggard digested this information.

Beth added, "You offered earlier that you would take points on notice, so we will make an appointment to return in two days. We want to know to whom you report in Randle and

Randle, and do you personally do any legal work for Mr Tony or Mrs Janine Matheson or family?"

Almost with relief, Hoggard quickly replied, "Definitely no! I would hardly recognise Tony Matheson myself, but I know our Senior Partner Paul Simperingham QC is a close friend and acts on his behalf. They may have gone to school and Uni together."

Linda expressed thanks for his time and responses so far, and repeated that they would be back to seek more information, particularly about the companies that appeared to be involved right from the beginning of the investigation. They would also be seeking more information on the two underage females and the older Filipina women involved in prostitution, e.g. where are their passports and work visas?

With perspiration now clearly visible on his forehead, Samuel Hoggard tried to calmly write a note for himself whilst visibly rattled. As the two police officers took their leave, Linda said that she would be talking again to the two Filipina women who were being held for questioning.

She added, "By the way, the body of Freda Zellerman's helper at Williamstown has been discovered. It seems someone didn't want anyone to hear anything from Wiremu Williams."

Several weeks later, and just before Beth was due to depart the police team, Linda decided she would take Helen Murphy along with her to another meeting as her assistant, to make up part of her police induction. As there was no great expectation of new evidence, her inexperience would not be an issue.

Linda suggested to Helen she should first ask Beth about

the best approach and demeanour to assume in the meeting.

Helen did ask, and Beth advised, "Listen and watch, keep your lips locked and let it all roll on." She added that DS Alexander sometimes used unorthodox methods and ruses to elicit information about the mechanisms used in the acquisition and concealment of unlawful proceeds.

"It all sounds more complicated than it is," Beth assured Helen, but also warned her, "Don't crash into the conversation; be a fly on the wall."

The two Filipina women to be interviewed were being held in a low-security safe house, so the meeting was held there with a government-appointed interpreter present.

Linda began by informing the women they were not criminals and were unlikely to be prosecuted and sent to jail. The enquiry was mainly to establish with whom they were associated in Australia, and did they know where their passports were? The major surprise was that it quickly became evident they spoke and understood an amount of English. The interpreter was a hawk-faced, smartly dressed woman who looked as though she would tolerate no nonsense, as if she had heard it all before.

The discussion was held in a low-key fashion with Linda and Helen dressed in smart civilian clothes to avoid any intimidation from police uniforms.

Linda's first question was, "Is your welfare in order?" That provoked looks of bewilderment from them that the interpreter established meant that they did not understand the term.

Linda then asked, "Are you being treated properly?" and this helped clarify the question. The response was 'all ok'.

A new question from Linda was, "Are you comfortable about your safety?" then "Please explain how you came to be locked up in Williamstown."

Helen threw in, "And who has been controlling you and locking you in your room?"

That elicited the immediate answer from both women, "Fredsie!" which, with the help of the interpreter, was easy to establish as Freda Zellerman. Especially when they went on in broken English to describe with humour all her tattoos. It was a good opportunity to explore whether they feared for their personal safety and whether they had considered trying to escape the confinement and the expectations of their 'work'.

The women admitted that they had not hatched any escape plans, mainly because of fear of retribution both locally and of repercussions from more serious criminal types who had controlled them from their own country. They were able to confirm they had arrived in Melbourne after a sea trip and although they had been promised generous wages and ultimately freedom and a passport, they had been bitterly disappointed, and were very depressed. They both turned to look directly at Linda with tears brimming in their eyes and although she remained visibly calm, Linda felt helpless to ease their distress or to offer any immediate relief.

She asked, "Who do you think is actually in charge?"

Without hesitation, both answered in unison, "Fredsie" again, waving their arms and hands around indicating her tattoos.

Did they know of, or had they ever met, a man called

Samuel Hoggard? The answer was no.

Helen helped to change the seating arrangements around to a more friendly shape so a softer atmosphere could evolve, to help get more details of events and functions the women had attended and how they had been paid or rewarded. It seemed they had been offered some drugs in lieu of cash but that was of no interest to them. They really had expected to be paid in money and they wanted to be free of their captors. Probably everyone in the room wondered, how could that ever be? Sadly, their lives were wrecked and no amount of platitudes the police might offer were likely to remedy that fact.

With the aid of the interpreter, the women asked how they could advance their case to improve their conditions and to commence positive steps to become 'Australians'. With some genuine sadness, Linda informed them that there were multiple steps to be taken before that was even a remote possibility. Suggestions from Helen about the appropriate government welfare agencies were welcomed and noted.

Shortly after, Linda closed the meeting with a polite, "Thank you to you both," and she and Helen returned to the police station.

In answer to questions on their progress, Linda described it as a 'work in progress', and Helen privately offered to Beth that, "It was a non-event, not a thing was achieved, and DI Alexander achieved nothing clever!"

Over a farewell glass of wine two days later, Beth passed on the comment to Linda and asked how it was all going. Linda suggested that she was now comfortable to concentrate on Freda Zellerman and to discover who the real movers and shakers were on the road to discovering the bigger picture. No need yet to over-inform Senior Constable Helen Murphy, although she planned to take her to help interview Freda Zellerman. Some sparks may fly.

Linda planned to take a uniformed sergeant to interview Samuel Hoggard in the office at Randle and Randle, Lawyers. That was proving to be harder than expected as it seemed he was playing hardball and not making himself available. Not a problem to Linda, as she simply went up the chain of seniority to a partner at the firm and thus a time and date was arranged for the next week to meet with Sam Hoggard.

She sent an outline agenda of subjects she wished to cover with Hoggard: Details of property ownerships as previously discussed; overseas experience, particularly London associates and records; Freda Zellerman and Ricky Russo, full details of relationships; Randle and Randle employment details, to whom Hoggard reported, and which partner was Hoggard's cousin; lifestyle, friends, and any overseas commercial contacts.

Linda received a formal acknowledgment that the agenda had been received, and she then arranged to take with her Inspector Ian McDonald to emphasise the seriousness of the follow-up discussion.

23

Art Show Drama

Two Lions Clubs based in the Kew area had planned for many months to hold their annual Art Show — which included sales and an auction — in the Town Hall. The format was to spread the event over a Saturday with the big range of paintings, photographs, sculptures, crockery etc that had been donated displayed around the large hall with suggested prices. The range included two or more major and valuable items to be sold as a silent auction and the final event was a major item to be sold in a 'live' auction at 7pm, before the event closed. All funds raised were to be donated to sporting facilities being built next to the Town Hall.

It was a very worthwhile and respectable community event and incorporated small musical recitals, tea cakes and coffee, and to which local and 'famous' personalities would attend as a show of support. Perhaps a tiny inclusion on TV news?

Meanwhile the two Filipina women taken into custody in Williamstown remained in the safe house with a policewoman appointed as carer. They were considered no risk, and were occasionally accompanied to safe events to be generous while the wheels of the law slowly turned. This day, the two women and carer were taken by taxi to the Art Show about 5pm, with a planned and approved timing to be back at 'home' before 7.30pm.

All went well until around 6pm when two well-dressed young men in black forcibly ushered the three out the front door of the hall into a strategically parked panel van. Little or no physical or voice resistance was given by the women. Shock, but no panic. They were driven off to a nearby quiet park where the men's sexual intent became obvious. It seemed they had no knowledge of the history of the young women as they tried roughly to remove their clothing. The carer they simply punched into silence, barking, "Shut your fucking mouth!"

However, the carer proved much tougher than expected and fought back, before jumping out and escaping, running away and screaming her lungs out. That attracted attention and the two potential rapists cursed and swore as they slammed the van doors and raced away with the two Filipina women. A witness had the presence of mind to record the van's rego. Because of the connection to the Williamstown event, the case of abduction quickly arrived on the desk of Inspector Linda Alexander.

Linda in turn delegated the case to Helen Murphy with the instruction, "Please keep me fully informed along the way."

Helen was pleased to be given an opportunity.

There were hundreds of white panel vans around the city, probably many with stolen rego plates. No one at the event recognised the men or the vehicle. Was it purely opportunistic or something else, she wondered?

Inquiries among known crooks and/or helpful police informants indicated no gang involvement. It was known to police that regular criminals hated this type of offence because of the unwanted police attention that followed. Senior Constable Murphy was excellent at kicking up a fuss.

In the meantime, the two men and their two hostages were in an apartment just off Brunswick Road, in Melbourne. They were not the smartest of criminals but did change the number plates on the panel van before parking it out on the street.

Helen sought help from Linda to stir up interest and assistance from the media, and to interview as many as possible attendees at the Lions Art Show. The fact that two senior police officers were actively pursuing the case attracted some additional interest from the media. It was hoped that the old police saying of, "squeeze it hard enough and something will come out," would prove true. It did prove to be partly true, as someone reported on a van that had not been moved for some days. With no noise or fuss, a police officer inspected the vehicle and reported that although locked, it did look as if there were some possible blood stains and some pieces of clothing visible.

Helen immediately got permission for entry to be made and hurried off to witness the event. It was established that there were blood stains and probable pieces of material in the van similar to the clothing worn by one of the women. Samples of the stains were taken to be compared with blood types of the three women.

Helen now homed in on likely accommodation for the two men they had descriptions of. With a uniformed police officer, Helen started the mundane routine of going door to door, shop to shop, and asking anyone on the street if they had seen either of the two suspects they were looking for. With enthusiasm and persistence, Helen would simply not accept a 'no' answer without being sure the question had been seriously considered.

Her perseverance really did succeed, as a woman walking her dog told her she thought a young man living in a local flat seemed to be a bit "shifty-eyed" in attitude, and was also buying large quantities of groceries and grog from the IGA supermarket. She had never seen him around before, and could also accurately tell them the building in which the suspect seemed to live.

Leaving nothing to chance, serious surveillance began, and within two days the officers were sure they had the suspects identified. With the help of DI Alexander and Chief Superintendent Brunton, the necessary protocols and permits were established so that Helen and associated uniformed officers could carry out a search warrant. The raid was carried out at 6am.

In spite of her own life experiences and background Helen, as the lead officer, was appalled at the scene they found. Both men were in underpants only, and looking unkempt and bleary-eyed. The two young women were almost naked, with ankles and wrists tied together, and tied down to heavy dining room chairs. They were heavily bruised, in bad shape physically, and almost certainly had been used brutally for sexual purposes.

They were terrified and hysterical.

Helen was beside herself with anger; when one of the men told her in no uncertain terms to, "Fuck off, before I use you too!" she showed great restraint in not responding as she called up Linda requesting medical and other police help immediately. She then, in the quietest possible way, told him to shut his smutty mouth and at the same time gave him the smoothest backhander the accompanying police officer had never seen, as the two apologies for human beings slunk back against the wall.

Helen was accorded congratulations for excellent police work. The dog walker was identified and invited in to receive a commendation for assisting community safety.

24
Worry in NZ

Meanwhile back in Hamilton, New Zealand, a storm was brewing in the Williams household as the family, including cousins and uncles, discussed the untimely demise of Wiremu, apparently in Melbourne. Officially, little or nothing had been notified to the family. Wiremu had always been a free spirit but as son and heir of substantial family holdings, respect and proper information about his death was expected and demanded. Wiremu's father was seriously ill and in no condition to pursue authorities, particularly in Australia. The family owned and operated a large earthmoving business and property in and around Mangere, just south of Auckland, with a staff of fifty.

The heated family discussions led to the appointment of Wiremu's sister, Elizabeth, (called Lizzie by everyone), to go to Melbourne to investigate what had happened. She was instructed not to be fobbed off by police or take any "Aussie bull dust!"

Lizzie duly arrived in Melbourne and booked herself into

the central Adina Apartments in Flinders Street. Unannounced, the well-spoken and educated Lizzie (Waikato University MA) started her inquiries at Williamstown Police Station. They were not very forthcoming with information but under persistent questioning confirmed the address of the home associated with Wiremu's last known activities, and suggested the names of Freda Zellerman, Ricky Russo, and particularly DI Linda Alexander as important contacts. Being the enterprising person she was, Lizzie quickly found their details and made contact with Freda.

Freda was reluctant to extend the telephone conversation with Lizzie, claiming she hardly knew Wiremu as he had been appointed to the job by gang people controlling the underage prostitutes' group, but she did volunteer the names of Ricky Russo and Sam Hoggard. She thought Wiremu was probably associated with the supply of drugs. That alone rang a bell for Lizzie as the rumour at home in New Zealand was that Wiremu was into drugs.

Hoggard was uncontactable and totally elusive. Contacts to Randle and Randle simply suggested she could leave messages to be forwarded on.

Ricky Russo, in his usual low-key friendly manner, agreed to meet for a coffee in Collins Street where he denied having ever met Wiremu. He agreed that he had been at functions that had been attended by the young women, but asserted that had only been as an invitee. He was bland and polite.

Lizzie by now was really stirring the criminal scene and her actions readily led to an appointment to meet Detective

Inspector Linda Alexander in her office. Linda was efficiently formal and prepared to listen as Lizzie explained the family concerns about lack of communication and the apparent lack of arrest. Linda was quietly assessing and admiring the impressive young women and her appeal for information, action and help.

There was good rapport established in the first few minutes that led to a not very satisfactory update. Details not previously published of how Wiremu's legs and ankles had been tied, which seemed to indicate that the murder was more serious and more like a message or revenge killing by heavy criminals, were passed on. The killing order clearly came from higher up the criminal hierarchy than from those organising simple prostitution. Lizzie put her hand to her mouth and gasped in distress. Very unusually for Linda, she rose from her chair and put her arm around Lizzie.

After a while, the conversation was renewed with a different level of empathy as Linda went on to provide a less detailed description of the wider crime scene being dealt with.

Lizzie knew the family would want to use all their resources to track down and retaliate in their own way for the crime. With sympathy Linda listened, and tried to discourage any thoughts of maverick revenge. She suggested an introduction for the family to Dennis Arkle, her equivalent police officer in Auckland, with the assurance that she would keep them up to date with progress, and as a trusted communication link. It did not seem to be much of a help but Wiremu had apparently been considered a potential leak of sensitive and serious information for a crime syndicate. Lizzie was appreciative of the information provided. Linda stressed the need for confidentiality as the investigation was in a critical stage. Lizzie knew this would not totally placate her family, and Linda almost begged her to be patient and restrain any revenge plans by her family. With Lizzie in her office Linda telephoned Inspector Arkle, asking him to help by visiting the family as soon as Lizzie returned.

Reluctantly Lizzie headed for home with assurances from Linda of ongoing contact.

25

Freda Zellerman

Because Freda Zellerman was both smart and tough, Linda decided she would be invited to the Police Station for the interview. Constable Helen Murphy would attend, and it would be formally recorded.

Freda arrived promptly, was greeted by Helen and led into the review room. They were joined by Linda, who formally introduced them all for the recording device.

Linda almost had to say to Helen, 'close your mouth; you look surprised!' as she admitted inwardly that Freda Zellerman looked as if she had stepped out of the film The Girl with the Dragon Tattoo. Introductions over, they proceeded with business.

Linda asked, "Are you OK if we call you Freda?" Freda nodded agreement.

Linda went on, "From our investigations both locally and particularly in London, you have both an informal police history and a formal criminal record, from being involved in prostitution and associations with crime syndicates. We are also aware that you were previously Miss Holloway, and from Northern Ireland. No record of a Mr Zellerman. You left London approximately three years ago."

"If you say so," Freda replied nonchalantly.

"It is obvious from the facts," said Linda, "that you were in charge of two underage females found wandering in Williamstown and two Filipina females under lock and key in premises at Williamstown."

No acknowledgement from Freda.

"Relative to those premises, you appear to be responsible for all activities and actions including those carried out by Ricky Russo," said Linda.

Freda exploded to her feet accompanied by many expletives, some of which even Helen had not been aware of, and screamed, "That's fucking bullshit!"

Calmly and in a low voice, Linda asked, "Which part of it are you referring to?"

Helen persuaded Freda to resume her seat.

Given the chance, Helen now somewhat provocatively offered, "Are you some kind of exhibitionist with your tattoos that are clearly meant to look like, but are not genuine, Maori? Or are you a member of some cult or bikie gang?"

It was not quite how Linda would have put it but it sufficed to produce an effect. Freda Zellerman raged and ranted for a while, then calm was restored. Linda restated that the main facts were known; the police knew about her past, and they now wanted details of her present employment. In particular, her relationship with Ricky Russo and Sam Hoggard and anyone else from whom she accepted instructions. Freda finally admitted that she and Russo were in a personal relationship — of no great stability — and also that she controlled the Williamstown property. Russo had the wider contacts, connections and involvements in various clubs and prostitution, and their activities overlapped and interlaced. Her instructions and communications for Williamstown came primarily through Sam Hoggard, and she knew that Hoggard in effect controlled Russo, probably on behalf of the top guys.

Linda asked, "Who would they be? Do you know who actually owns the property or boats?"

This simply led to genuinely blank looks from Freda.

Linda pushed hard to get from Freda names and addresses of her current contacts, and particularly contacts in the UK. However, all she would say was that the syndicates were so big and powerful that trying to hurt or infiltrate them would be like shooting toothpicks at an elephant. She, Freda, was not brave enough to contemplate any such action! Linda, in return, promised that all current actions undertaken by Freda would now be seriously curtailed, and recorded. The formal interview was drawing to a close.

A departing question from Linda was, "Do you know or have you met Mr and Mrs Tony Matheson? We think they may have attended some of the functions held on the yacht Pure Blue? They may have attended with Reggie McGuiness, the TV entrepreneur?"

Freda seemed to answer the question honestly, with a

shake of the head, although she thought she had heard of the Mathesons.

It was not mentioned to her that police surveillance had now been instituted on all the players involved in the case now called the 'Milly and Mandy affair'. Telephone intercepts, local and overseas encryptions, basic monitoring of all social habits and activities, and detailed examinations of past records and associates — at this stage all very low key and non-intrusive but very detailed.

There had not been a great outcome from the formal interview, thought Linda, but it would be useful for other discussions.

26
Samuel Hoggard

Some of the detail from Freda Zellerman's interview could be used in the planned re-interview of Sam Hoggard — this time at the police station — and he was deliberately made to wait in the foyer to be exposed to the full police atmosphere. The formal interview was held in a plain room with little space after DI Linda Alexander and Inspector Ian McDonald spread their files over the small boardroom table. They informed Sam that it was a formal interview and was being recorded. No need as yet for him to be accompanied by a solicitor.

As previously advised, they would run through the formal agenda. Ownership of the premises in Williamstown, and other premises used as nightclubs, his overseas relationships including any family, details of who he reported to at Randle and Randle, Lawyers. An elaboration of his personal Melbourne lifestyle including memberships of all clubs and groups. There was a gap in information about company ownerships, as his previous answers were that they were shell companies.

Hoggard tried to be both evasive but at the same time a typically professional lawyer, giving away nothing. It was established early on that his contact at the legal firm was his cousin Matthew Merriweather, a senior partner.

Linda did allow a vague reference to police use of sophisticated surveillance equipment into the interview to try to unsettle Hoggard. Ian McDonald pushed him hard, asking about Freda Zellerman and Ricky Russo each reporting separately to him, and yet seeming to be one team. Ian suggested that perhaps there were two different masters on two different projects, maybe overlapping?

Hoggard quipped, "what devious minds you have!"

Linda wanted to strengthen the point. "We have extensive recordings, from and to all parties in this saga, and intend to take prosecutions to the nth degree. We have interviewed Freda Zellerman at length and believe we are right up to speed with her history and involvement. We are doing the same soon with Ricky Russo and his uncle Paul Wheeler, and expect to extract more information."

The two police officers went on to repeat to Sam Hoggard how sophisticated police surveillance had now become. They reiterated to him recent successes using drones, telephone and video tapping, and Customs successes with the tracing of large shipments of drugs and particularly cocaine from Europe, secreted in various products and refrigerated containers. Agencies all around the world were beginning to work together to stop illicit drug importation and to ultimately arrest the final distributors.

Their message was loud and clear: much was being done to stop or disrupt the organised criminals who had no concern for the scourge of illicit drugs or their impact upon societies. They commented how it had been alleged that local motor bike gangs were closely associated with international members and the point was made that all connections were being traced.

27

Ricky Russo

The entire police team allocated to solving the crimes associated with the Milly-Mandy case, were now spreading their nets far and wide in unusual areas including overseas and border controls. Every type of enquiry was put into action. Superintendent Ron Brunton was coordinating the activities and liaised regularly with Linda. When informed of the plan to interview Ricky Russo he immediately offered to do some sleuthing through police records to help. Armed with the records, Linda invited Helen Murphy to accompany her to interview Ricky.

The introductions were polite and Ricky was neat and tidy in smart casual clothes. He had short black hair and a finely trimmed small moustache. Immediately, Linda thought to herself that he looked like a well-polished criminal.

Her first question was, "We know you liaise and communicate regularly with Samuel Hoggard of Randle and Randle, so do you have any other bosses that you report to?"

Politely but quickly, Ricky responded, "what the hell does that mean?"

Linda said, "To be fair, we have done a lot of research on you and at best we can only describe you as an 'opportunistic mid-level local criminal' who probably edges into drugs and prostitution when the chances arrive. We know about activities in and around Exhibition Street, Melbourne, and of course your relationship with Freda Zellerman. So again, I ask: apart from direct or indirect instructions from Sam Hoggard, do you work for other masters?"

Not being particularly experienced or tough, or even an actor, Ricky fluffed around trying to avoid the question. Under further pressure, he did admit to working as a pimp in more than one brothel and said he was employed by the owners. He volunteered the name already well known to police. Helen continued to provoke and stir him, and he admitted he had on occasions delivered drugs to or for some bikie gangs. Helen enjoyed the chance to be inquisitive and found Ricky quite entertaining in a basic way. He was happy to claim he had contacts in the jazz and nightclub music scene.

Linda needed to get back to her main subject, and asked, "Do you by any chance know, or have you met, Tony and Janine Matheson, who may have attended functions on the yacht Pure Blue; they may have been accompanied by TV star and entrepreneur Reggie McGuiness?

Ricky replied, "That's easy! The Mathesons I do not know personally, but I have seen them sometimes in Williamstown at various restaurants with McGuiness, who is just a big showoff. Tony Matheson, I believe, is very well respected."

Ricky was quite enjoying the attention from the police

officers and went on to comment, "My life is a bit like my favourite music..."

Helen was quick to enquire, "And what would that be?"

"I lay down on a bed of roses, and woke up lying on a bed of nails. Singer Bon Jovi," Ricky answered as he looked around for approval from the officers.

Was he just a fool, or much deeper than he appeared, Linda asked herself?

In an effort to get back to the main enquiry, Linda asked him again, "What about your associations with the yacht Pure Blue, and Bella Companions, Agile Athletes, and the various gym clubs and brothels in Melbourne?"

She asked again if there were interconnections between the company personnel and the activities of any gangs? A blank look from Ricky.

Helen asked, "Are you involved in the supply of drugs?" This was where Ricky illustrated his nimbleness of tongue and mind and avoided questions or just ignored them.

Linda reverted to questions about Sam Hoggard, and company ownership details, but again drew a blank from Ricky. To the question of who he knew within Randle and Randle, he said the only other person he had met was a Matthew Merriweather. Ricky thought that Sam and Matthew might be working together there.

Other questions on which Linda asked Helen to contribute were on the subjects of cybercrime and extortion through the use of ransom payments to release a hostage. Russo knew about how it all worked but had never been involved.

He said he was well aware of the dark web and its uses.

Much the same information that had been given to Hoggard to illustrate police sophistication in drug tracing was passed on to Russo to reinforce the police's serious intent.

Helen enjoyed her participation in the discussion and was more than competent in contributing. Her police training, experiences with people, the new stability in her home life, were all adding to the growing confidence she portrayed in her position as a police officer. The formal interview finished and Ricky Russo departed.

The next day Linda invited Helen for a coffee at the morning tea break, with the aim of reassuring her that she was doing well. Deputy Ian McDonald was well aware of the tactic and the encouragement being given to Helen. There was a constant lookout kept for any chinks in the junior officer's armour, to be able to step in and assist.

28

Review. Helen Murphy: Assessment

Back in police HQ the incident room was busy with more research, reviews, and repeated re-reading of every piece of evidence gathered. The major question to Linda seemed to be, how big a cog in the crime syndicate was Sam Hoggard? That answer, quite surprisingly, took a giant leap forward when a UK police connection came forward to disclose more information — back through Sam's cousin, senior Randle and Randle partner Matthew Merriweather, who had a brother in London. Reputedly, as relayed by UK police, the brother in London was a millionaire entrepreneur and playboy, known for his global polo and rugby connections, a reputation for ostentatious behaviour, and total disregard for other people's feelings.

International help with appropriate discretion was requested. The rumour was that the same London entrepreneur had connections in New Zealand with a well-established Auckland businessman of doubtful repute.

Almost on an impulse, Linda arranged a short sharp

visit to Auckland to run over a variety of points relating to drug imports, the involvement of bikies on both sides of the Tasman, the combining of surveillance in transit and better use of cyber technology. One of her main reasons was to explore with her counterpart Inspector Dennis Arkle the likelihood of an Auckland 'Mr Big' criminal associated or connected to the Merriweather brother in London. Dennis Arkle was positive there was a London connection who used encrypted communications and thought the Merriweather brother was a good lead.

Other criminal activities of commonality to both police forces were discussed, and the now serious growth of cocaine importation was of particular concern. Money laundering was common but the scale was not so grand in the smaller New Zealand population. So-called 'rat-lists' were known. The ingenuity of methods used to bring in and distribute drugs was always expanding and changing. Genuine antiques, ethnic carvings, paintings, canned fruit, the use of unsuspecting 'gofers', specially built pipes and tubes in machinery, were all common in NZ. The threat of physical violence to ensure secrecy was becoming ever more common.

A good exchange of views ensued; Linda had kept the communication current and had confirmed the likelihood of a Merriweather syndicate connection, so there were no surprises. The theory that communications and stock movements could easily be shuffled around the London/Australia/NZ triangle, or even wider to thwart authorities, was discussed. Australia and NZ sent requests for information about the Merriweather

London modus operandi back to London police.

Back in Melbourne, a small staff issue had arisen. Sensible police officer that he was, Inspector Ian McDonald asked for a private word with Linda to discuss Helen Murphy. A great respecter of protocol and fairness, Ian asked if this could be off the record, but listened to carefully. Linda immediately assured him of her unfailing trust in his judgement and personal support.

Ian said, "You have only been away four days so my judgement may be suspect, but although Constable Murphy is undoubtedly very intelligent, in my opinion she may be dangerous."

He waited for a moment or two, but Linda did not respond as she waited for him to go on, which he did: "You know she can be disruptive and is always prodding and poking at everyone's personality. She never eases up. She has the type of ego that has to score points in every situation. Always challenging! She hasn't a clue about team building, and is totally unsympathetic to ideas that others volunteer. In fact she is quite the opposite, constantly putting down other contributions with overbearing questions and comments. And constant interruptions."

A few deep breaths from Ian, who was clearly extremely distressed at having to be so negative. Linda encouraged him to go on.

"Linda, you know me well enough, and I enjoy my job, but there is a problem here. Every pleasant incident or moment that has been quietly building up team enjoyment, within minutes or even over days she can and does undo with a withering 'downer'. She is a malcontent. It seems to me she always wants to be noticed and acknowledged. 'Look at me, look at me.' She really is not a team player, and she has the habit of hitting back with a thousand words — to pay back with interest. Her irritation is showing through and her obvious anger has frightened some junior staff."

He went on to add that the classic apparently had been when she had very rudely said to another constable, "don't interrupt me — I'm reading. Now go away and get yourself organised before you try to talk to me again!"

Clearly trying to be fair, Ian added that he was aware she had been a teacher, and maybe was used to pushing kids around, and again maybe she had problems at home in Brunswick, but she had clearly never heard of, 'Let it go through to the keeper and protect team spirit'.

Another deep breath, then, "Linda, we really do need to address this."

Linda Alexander was not usually a swearer but now said, "Bloody hell, Ian, this is awful. Got any recommendations?"

As the serious police officer that he was, Ian took his time to elaborate on the broader situation as he perceived it.

"Good quality investigative officers are few and far between. Helen is clearly highly intelligent and mature enough to make an excellent detective. She is erudite, well groomed, athletic, and presents well. All these factors could help her to be successful in the police force. So, to be fair to her, are we missing something from her background?"

All Linda could add was that she had arrived strongly supported from 'within police'.

Ian pressed on, trying to help and to forcefully impress on Linda the need to intervene immediately. He suggested that a staff rebellion may be imminent. Linda realised the gravity of the situation and asked Ian to talk to the team on a one-on-one basis, while she promised that she would call Helen in for counselling and obtain a transfer for her, if needed.

The meeting between Linda and Helen seemed to proceed well enough as Linda conducted the session first thing the next morning. She stressed the need for good team morale and respect for all opinions within the team culture. Helen seemed to receive the general feedback well. The session took over an hour and as Linda had a scheduled appointment to see Ricky Russo, she decided to invite Helen to accompany her. That also seemed to go well and gave Linda further opportunities to measure Constable Murphy.

Linda revisited, for the benefit of Russo, the concerns she had about his depth of criminality locally. She again asked him about his connections with any bikie gangs and money laundering through various pubs and clubs. She suggested and repeated that his involvement in prostitution, consorting and associated violent crime, made him a prime suspect to be involved in syndicated crime. Linda added that he did not appear on the surface to be a vicious, hardnosed, international criminal.

Ricky's assuredness and arrogance surfaced a few times but there was a rapport that had quickly developed between Helen and Russo, which Linda recognised.

Afterwards, Linda invited Helen to have a light lunch with

her where she took the opportunity to broach again the subject of behaviour, this time more forcefully and in greater detail.

Things did not proceed smoothly this time and Helen made some silly, wild, shallow accusations as she could not contain her anger. Partly as appeasement and as encouragement for an in-depth more honest discussion, Linda expressed admiration for Helen's skills and prospects for advancement.

The result of that, surprisingly, was to set Helen off in a tirade of anger and resentment, and she almost spat out, "You know you are not doing your job well! In fact, I should have your job and it would be done more quickly and efficiently. It won't happen of course, because I don't have a fair chance. I'm always being picked on!"

Linda could not let that continue so she interrupted, "Wow! wow! You're welcome to express your opinion but we're getting a long way from the reason for this chat, which is to voice concern re your lack of appreciation of others' contributions to the team culture, and our reason to be. In case you missed the point, that is solving serious syndicated crime."

The words flowed back and forth with little or no change in attitude from Helen, so finally Linda sent her back to work with the immediate task of urgent and in-depth investigation into Ricky Russo, including associates internationally. Helen scoffed a little as she agreed to do so but offered the opinion, "He is nothing more than a mid-level gofer for those who pay him well and who terrify him."

Linda said, "Well, that's a start, so be quick to prove it."

A few days later Linda was having one of her irregular 'cup

of tea chats' with her boss Superintendent Brunton about things in general and she mentioned in passing that she had spoken to Constable Murphy about her negative effect on team morale.

In his laconic, laid-back manner, Brunton said, "Yes, I am aware of it. She crashed into my office a week or two ago complaining about the police force in general, but I sent her on her way." Linda looked at him and waited for elaboration.

All he added was, "What a pity, what a waste of time. I told her to look for a new position that suited her talents, whatever they were."

29
Russo Re-interview

Harmony did not return easily to the highly motivated police team that Linda and Ian McDonald had patiently built, and for a short period every one tiptoed around the 'Helen problem'. It was agreed that Ian would take Constable Murphy to pursue one more opportunity to extract information from Ricky Russo, who was becoming a highly rated suspect rather than merely a lightweight charmer. He seemed to have the ability not to be seen or heard, a harmless invisible middle man. It was now a little over a month since the police team's near rebellion and the tactic agreed between Ian and Helen was to ask Russo about low-key associations within a gang culture and how to remain invisible while participating.

A meeting was arranged, and when the questions were put to him, Ricky scoffed at such propositions and suggested he was being misjudged. Ian corrected that by suggesting the phrase was "under-estimated". It was all conducted in a relaxed fashion, and then Helen began to aggressively pursue the subject of the penalties for procurement of underage females for prostitution, and the locking up of alleged victims. There were strong denials of any involvement from Russo but Helen put on a show of her deep knowledge of the law.

Ian finished the interview along the lines of the police research homing in on contacts and connections between Melbourne lawyers and international criminals — all being part of syndicates active in drugs and money laundering. The money trail, he said, was proving to be illuminating. He dropped into the conversation that the association between Ricky Russo and lawyer Sam Hoggard was creating attention. A final word to Ricky was that he was 'a person of interest' and was not to leave Melbourne.

Ian said to Ricky, "We are aware that you and Freda Zellerman have a casual sexual friendship, and you apparently report separately to different bosses. That is going to cost you both dearly, either jointly or separately." He would not elaborate.

On the way back to the station, Helen lost her composure and suggested to Ian that the police force and the OCS division in particular were incompetent. She said in the heat of the moment that she had no respect for Ian, and even less for DI Linda Alexander, and that she wanted a transfer. All said in very angry tones, and listened to by Ian in silence. Ian, of course, dutifully reported this to Linda with his brief and simple recommendation: "Let's waste no more time on her. She must go."

Not without a few ructions occurring within the team, it was decided the best and simplest way for Constable Helen Murphy to exit was to be taken up through levels of seniority and then finally left for Superintendent Brunton to authorise the departure. On the surface the official police notification was non-acrimonious but anger all round within ranks was obvious.

Of interest was that in the interim period prior to the effective date of termination, and while on suspension from all police duties, Helen was secretly observed in the company of Ricky Russo, apparently doing a tour of some of the notorious premises that Russo was known to supervise. Premises such as Flingtasia, Club Q, and the associated premises in Russell Street. Even more interesting to the police was the observation of a much more clandestine threesome lunching in a back room — a group of Helen Murphy, Ricky Russo and Sam Hoggard. A little later they were observed to be surreptitiously joined by no other than the radio shock jock Reggie McGuiness. However, the police observers were only casual and were certainly not experienced cybersecurity engineers with high-tech equipment and thus there was no chance to eavesdrop.

In formally farewelling Helen, Superintendent Brunton briefly wished her well and reminded her of the documents she had signed when she joined the force. Several weeks after her departure a report arrived on the desk that he shared with Inspector Linda Alexander, that Russo was now observed as a regular visitor, including overnight, at the home of Helen Murphy. The judgement was that it was clearly a sexual relationship and there was even a suggestion that one or other had recruited the other. They agreed it was not a real worry that Helen possessed any great police secrets of any progress being made in the bigger picture of the international crime syndicate operating from or through Melbourne.

30
Alliance

The Murphy-Russo-Hoggard alliance sparked renewed attention on the family connection through solicitor Matthew Merriweather and the London family. Linda was sure the scale and size of the criminality involved many participants outside those already identified. She was looking for a local 'Mr Big' who was powerful, but not all-powerful. The money involved was huge, and most of it revolved around drugs. The latest alert had come from informed sources that a major supply route was through armed forces personnel with subsequent extensive distribution through bikie gangs.

Linda contacted her associate Dennis in New Zealand to check if they were getting similar feedback there, and they confirmed that their supply was through RNZAF personnel at the Whenuapai air base. The close associates were bikies who also had become expert in money laundering, and who held a lot of the criminality together with the use of fear and physical harm. The Auckland scenario was more difficult as they had identified their own Mr Big who seemed to be involved everywhere; he had migrated from Scotland to NZ about fifteen years ago. It seemed unlikely there was a London relationship.

The OCS team worked tirelessly and were able to dissect the petty crime from the ugly, much larger crime. Much of the digging was associated with the Australian Federal Police who had much longer tentacles embraced all the lawyers, mafia connections, drugs and money launderers — all of whom used an anonymous decoded encrypted message transferring system. Their so-called 'trusties' who helped the criminals were also legally employed at ports and airports handling freight. Working on the sidelines these people were generously rewarded and were mainly unaware that police surveillance was gradually bringing them into focus. Their lawyers — who fringed into illegal areas — were also being closely monitored, even to the extent of having all their correspondence analysed, not just for drugs but for wider connections.

A new phenomenon in local criminal activity was the strong and aggressive growth of what were called 'professional' Vietnamese criminals, active in money laundering particularly at large pokies venues. The rivalry between bikie gangs and other enforcers was local, but had international connotations.

Linda and her team were confident there were significant connections through Samuel Hoggard, Matthew Merriweather and his London-based connections. All the local police checking had indicated that Randle and Randle, Lawyers, as an entity was clean and that senior partner Paul Simperingham was beyond doubt also clean.

The police summary of radio personality Reggie McGuiness was that he seemed to be everywhere, was also a TV star, but commercially was considered a lightweight. Reggie was a local boy who had done well, and was popular with the public in many different spheres as he donated both money and his personal time to raise awareness and funds for underprivileged families. A confidential enquiry was instigated into his assets and wealth. Was he connected to Williamstown or other properties?

31
New 'Team'

Unknown to Linda or her team, Helen Murphy and Freda Zellerman had been introduced to one another by Ricky Russo as potential members of the same group and as active partners, attempting to maximise its raison d'etre. Details, or the consequences, had not been thought through by Ricky. Visually, the two could hardly have been less similar. Helen still looked like a school teacher but even more like a well-presented conservative police constable. Her neat, short-trimmed blonde hair, comfortable walking shoes and minimal makeup contrasted sharply with Freda's exotic tattoos, colourful apparel and multi-coloured hair, and made them an unlikely couple, although it had to be noted that Freda could modify her appearance for an occasion by wearing long sleeves and a skirt. Exception often proves the rule and quite quickly the two found enough in common to enjoy each other's company, and to smile together when people stared. It was not long before reports of them being seen together filtered back to Linda and team, creating speculation about the possible significance.

Although not formally recorded nor videoed by police surveillance, the hours the young women spent together shopping in the department stores in central Melbourne, with coffee then a light lunch in the European Café in Spring Street, provided a wonderful opportunity for them to get to know each other. Subjects ranged freely from food to cosmetics to travel, sex and everything in between.

Freda surprised Helen by announcing she was a vegan. To add emphasis, she added the quote, "I am grateful to realise that my desires do not entitle me to add to another's suffering." She wanted to chat more about diet but was content to wander among the shops and enjoy some retail therapy with Helen. Their discussions covered the usual likes and dislikes about products they passed, and Freda — with her extensive tattoos — was almost silent on the subject of skin care and cosmetics. On questions from Helen about the vegan diet, Freda was happy to elaborate on the extremes she had been to, and all she had tried, to look fit and trim. They complimented each other on how fit and athletic the other looked, knowing the work and effort entailed. They each admitted that they had been down the roads of fasting, raw paleo, prescription and illegal drugs, you name it — all in the endeavour to be fit and to look good. Great to laugh about as they wandered idly among the expensive merchandise. As an aside, Freda admitted to Helen that she had at one stage of her career been a skilled shoplifter. Over a light lunch Helen asked if the tattoos meant membership in a gang, club, or organisation?

Freda's answer was, "No, not really, I just fancied the idea of body art, and they grew bigger and better with encouragement from the crowd I mixed with. We all fancied ourselves as toughies and graduated aimlessly into crime. That was back at home."

The relaxed atmosphere led to Helen confiding that she had been a member of a cult. Freda almost gulped as she asked, "What sort of a group was it?" Helen told her it was a little-known group called NXIVM. She was reasonably sure Freda would not have heard of it. With little encouragement Helen determinedly set about enlightening her. "You probably wouldn't know much about my chequered past but I'll give you a brief resume to pass the time while we enjoy our 'getting to know you'."

Helen went on, "For many years I was a primary school teacher, and that gave me time to study and learn for myself. One of the things that sparked my curiosity was cults of varying styles and intensities. I looked at Scientology and the man named Hubbard, probably because of film-star connections, but I was scared off by the Charles Manson group's history and other fanatical orders. Most of them seemed to have 'family' and 'religious' connotations, and a basic "droit du seigneur" or Lord's right, which simply means the leader, always a man, holds supposed legal or customary rights like a feudal lord over his flock. You can just imagine what that meant in a sexual sense." Helen emphasised all that with a wry smile. Then she added that the group that really got her attention was NXIVM.

Helen then generously asked if Freda would like to have her chance to talk more about some of the weird diet tried, or maybe just a short simple summary about NXIVM, both subjects to be elaborated on later if of real interest?

Freda enthusiastically opted for more about the mysterious cult as she exclaimed, "Never heard of it!" The relaxed discussion was expanding the friendship into a confessional.

The freedom of exchange was not disrupted even when Helen looked directly at a tattoo and pointedly asked Freda, "Have you been in goal?"

Without even a blink Freda replied, "As a matter of fact I have, back in England; why?"

Calmly and with a little superiorly, Helen offered, "It seems to be a likelihood of probability!" They both laughed long and loud. Keeping it brief, Helen went on to outline a little about the cult of NXIVM. In essence it was an American sex cult that attracted brainwashed women into being its 'slaves'. It was promoted as a self-improvement group run by the charismatic leader Keith Raniere. The group attracted many high-profile actors pushing the old dogma "Universal truths about how to improve yourself and how to look closer at things." Helen realised she had lost Freda's attention and so suggested they resume their shopping. They wandered back through David Jones and began heading for home.

They parted to make their own ways home after a day that had established a closer relationship with no harm done — as they had both observed a very old saying, 'In life, and in social conversation, never lift heavy stones unnecessarily'. Helen hurried home to Brunswick where she relaxed and contemplated her new relationship.

32
Intuition

Back in the OCS special projects room, the team were summarising and communicating the position as to achieving arrests and prosecution for their prime objective, which had commenced with the two young girls obviously lost in the streets of Williamstown. The targets were now much wider, including international crime syndicates that roamed freely from product to product and country to country, as easily as making an encrypted anonymous communication. The need for criminal leadership at each venue was obvious.

The walls displayed photos, diagrams and quotes covering subjects quite randomly. DI Linda Alexander relished the challenge even though she felt frustration about progress in identifying the real heavies operating in Melbourne. Her well-tuned intuition kept assuring her that the solicitor Samuel Hoggard was an integral part of illegal activities, but not the big brawn or brains of the local scene. She was sure there was

As a keen and capable tennis player she analysed her responsibilities as in a serious tennis game. What was the key? Did the leader have an obvious big serve that commanded fear and respect from all the other players? No one stood out like the proverbial dog's balls. The purpose of the game was to make obscene big money through crime. So where were the foot faults and disputed line calls? It was obvious to Linda that the after-event thanks, to 'the umpire and ball boys' were more than generous enough to keep them all very happy. There were no obvious cracks.

Her intuition and experience kept nagging her to go back up the ladder and relook. Who was the coach that could teach new skills like under spins, top spins, mental toughness, and new techniques, to those who might dramatically improve? The rewards had to be huge to offset the risks. Onshore or offshore leadership; so where is Mr Big?

Linda reflected that Sam Hoggard was no doubt a crook and had connections back to the legal world in London. He had no entrepreneurial skills, he seemed to her to be just a skilled lawyer who had been caught up in some shonky deals — no obvious great leadership skills there. When Linda gave the subject more thought, the name Reggie McGuiness kept leaping to the front of her mind. And who was his close social friend within the club scene, and probably other areas, but Ricky Russo.

The search of the Ricky Russo persona, which had become almost an obsession for second in charge Ian McDonald, now began to provide results. It was soon obvious that over the years

Ricky had been a successful drug dealer who always seemed to keep himself just beyond the level of serious police interest. The background summary produced the intelligence that he was a well-presented young man who for many years had lived with his parents in Sydney Road in Melbourne, not long after they had immigrated from London. Ricky had spent part of his teen years within earshot of Bow Bells, East London, and he had contemporary friends there.

His education in Melbourne had been unspectacular and included two visits with his parents back to the UK. It was widely assumed in Australia that with the surname Russo he was Italian but both his parents were English. As a young man, being slim, neat, well dressed and with a slight 'pommy' accent, Ricky could have been whatever he chose. He drifted into catering, coffee shops and entertainment. He was well liked and respected and could be relied on. The supply and use of illegal drugs was common. Possessing both a high IQ and the right social contacts, it occurred to Ricky that some old friends and contacts in London could point him in the right direction for wholesale drugs. It took a while but by his late twenties he was underway. More than just drugs, he also established a confidential relationship with a 'family' of greater consequence. It evolved that his uncle Paul Wheeler was part of a group that could not be penetrated, that had been woven together internationally.

It was of great surprise to Ian McDonald. Part of the probable outcome was an ever-growing list of assets that could residences in Gardenvale in Melbourne, both leased out on long-term contracts, were owned by Ricky's mother Giulia Russo, operating from an address in Sydney Road, Carlton. Also, a holiday home in Queenscliff and a similar property in Maroochydore in Queensland. Both properties were in leasing rental pools and in the name of Ricky's father. Ricky's parents both drove late-model Subaru SUVs and kept very low-key appearances. Ricky had his own luxury apartment in Collingwood in Melbourne, but still spent much time with his parents. He drove a blue Holden Berlina kept in immaculate order. The ownership of the upmarket Collingwood property was shrouded in trusts and shell companies, plus share portfolios also hidden within shell company names.

Ricky was a low-level socialite, occasionally appearing with glamorous females but who were not judged as his permanent companions. He comfortably mixed with all levels of society and appeared to be in the group most often associated with Reggie McGuiness. It was not often commented on, but they were chalk and cheese. Reggie, with outgoing, gregarious ways, a notable leader who loved the limelight. Ricky, with his low key, genuinely charming ways, was a quiet achiever. He was quick with words and had a soft humour that was easy to undervalue. Ricky's favourite saying was seemingly about toothache: 'The pain that leads to extraction'.

To Ian and Linda, Ricky seemed the perfect journeyman— the one person all could rely on and always there. Could he be the potential chink in the armour?

Reggie McGuiness had his own small PR company and staff

team based in a rental office in Lygon Street, Carlton. RMG and Associates Ltd it was named. Not all its activities were purely public relations. Two part-time efficient staff were called his 'support team' and were tough to bypass. They ran his diary and coordinated and controlled all his commercial activities.

Another member of the RMG team was a more serious and mysterious individual. John Silverman was a behind-the-scenes authority and apparently a retired lawyer who had arrived in Australia twenty-five years ago from England. He had worked with and for Reg McGuiness for the past fifteen years. Silverman was by nature a back-room operator and his plump, slightly dishevelled and swarthy appearance was in stark contrast to the smooth, well-groomed figure of Reggie McGuiness.

Both in demeanour and in his physical looks, John Silverman was not true to his name; in fact, he had an extremely ugly nature. He had occasionally accompanied Reggie on overseas trips and was a regular traveller on his own. Silverman was a powerful person with a low public profile. He was considered a 'Mr Fixit' — a member of established clubs, a registered political lobbyist, and often consulted by companies seeking influence. He was unfriendly and aloof to all and could be very cruel to those he considered inferior to himself.

33

Clever Plan

Through the depth of the police connections came a super-confidential tipoff. The whisper was that a plan for a massive shipment of mixed drugs into Australia was underway in Europe. No names, no pack drill as yet. The plan involved the use of products from a not so known museum in a mid-sized European city that was repatriating quantities of Polynesian, NZ, and Australian Aboriginal artifacts.

Preliminary approvals, permits and government authorisations were underway, and the registered trader was discovered to be a little company from Bosnia. The suggestion was that the artifacts, tools and other historical effects were to be shipped via Fiji, Auckland, and finally to Melbourne. It all seemed like a feasible plan. The timing was unknown at this stage but Linda immediately contacted her friend and associate Inspector Dennis Arkle in Auckland to enquire in the most confidential manner, whether he had heard the slightest murmur of such a possibility? Dennis was pleased to hear from Linda as they had established a comfortable working relationship and a personal and professional respect.

Dennis agreed there had been some very early murmurings of a clever and complicated deal being hatched through international connections. No detail and no information about artifacts. He thanked Linda and gave her an assurance that he would respect the confidential information and would continue to share communications with her.

Linda reflected on some of the reasons why people disclosed, or leaked, confidential information they knew they had been trusted with.

Some people were just 'leakers' and were mean, bitter and twisted in themselves, and it was done to witness the damage. Sometimes it happened when there had been a perceived insult done to someone, or they perceived themselves to have been overlooked, or were offended by not being chosen to use the new wonder toy or the latest model something; there was the bypassed promotional opportunity, the non-inclusion in the senior group allowed to share in prestige; missing out on being nominated for something — the reasons could be many and varied. Often it could be because of bitter internecine warfare, just below the surface. And the most common reason of all: crossed relationships, sexual and non-sexual, including actions for payback, and to compensate for perceived humiliation. Tame journalists played their parts.

For some, a little harm can be justified by an old philosophy, "I'll do a little good to allow a little bad," or "A little bad can be offset by a little

Linda and her team were constantly examining the many possible motivations to lure in information.

The close relationship enjoyed between the OCS and the AFP existed partly because of normal regular professional contacts, but also because Linda had several more personal contacts within the AFP that made for good communications. It was confirmed that the antiques and artifacts were legitimate articles being shipped and identified on the ship's manifest, with deliveries scheduled to a variety of destinations according to the origin of the articles. The ownership had been controversial but apparently the right of return had been agreed by the countries involved.

The vessel was not a 'tramp steamer' but formally registered in Panama and carrying general cargo with accommodation for up to twenty passengers. The vessel, the MV Handymax, was classified as a twin decker of around 20,000 tonnes with multi-purpose lifting gear useful at small ports. The manifest included one caretaker from the museum who was responsible for the safe transit of the articles. He was named as Esad Hodzic of Sarajevo, described as a historian. The recorded planned ports of call included Gibraltar, the Panama Canal, Galapagos Islands, Rarotonga, Fiji, Vanuatu, Port Moresby, Auckland and Brisbane. Surreptitious inspection of the manifest revealed nothing suspicious about any of the passengers, they all appeared to be ordinary tourists. The elderly captain was respected, and the crew seemed mainly of Pakistani heritage. Subtle monitoring of the voyage was put into operation and nothing untoward was anticipated, nor did it evolve.

Several unofficial raids and inspections were made of the products in the holds and nothing suspicious or illegal was discovered. Over many weeks the MV Handymax progressed along its reported route. At each of the designated ports of call there was an official welcome as the artifacts were unloaded, often accompanied by pomp and ceremony provided by local dignitaries — presidents or prime ministers and sometimes including a Chinese diplomat.

Little or no pick-up trade was involved until the ship reached Fiji. The captain was aware that there was cargo to be picked up with some of it scheduled for Vanuatu and Auckland, and the majority for Brisbane. It consisted of large quantities of what was apparently famous Fijian artesian drinking water, all wrapped in clear outer plastic bubbles on wooden pallets; easy to load and store. The voyage progressed at a leisurely pace through calm seas to Auckland where a large quantity of the artifacts was unloaded and customs and police gave the products a detailed inspection, even using specialist sonar equipment. Nothing untoward was discovered. Esad Hodzic, the historian, left the vessel in Auckland and flew home to Sarajevo as there was only a small number of artifacts left bound for Australia. The vessel was picking up products to take to Europe and anticipated more 'pickups' from Australia.

Linda wondered if false information had been planted, or was an organisation trying out the accuracy of information given or received to create false leads?

Without incident, the MV Handymax proceeded to Brisbane

artesian water consignment. Intact in the original bubble wrap, the water was consigned on to a warehouse in Collingwood. Ricky knew all about it but Freda did not.

34

Message Interceptions

With persistent monitoring, Linda's team had a significant breakthrough listening in to the telephones of the suspects. Even more importantly, the methods of communication being used from London became known and hacked into by police. John Silverman, the apparent backroom operator for Reggie McGuiness and operating from the office in Lygon Street, Carlton, was in regular communication with London, always using encryptions. It had also become apparent that Silverman was probably the senior operator in Victoria and that Ricky Russo reported to him.

The depth and sophistication of the group became more evident when it was detected that one of the ways of communicating offshore was through an agent buried in Bishop Court in the Anglican Trinity Church complex in Clarendon Street, East Melbourne. He had worked as an administrative assistant for years and had the anonymous use of many facilities.

Fitzroy or Treasury Gardens, or along the road at the Pullman Hotel were great places for secretive meetings or exchange of official — and otherwise — data.

It became known that 'they' had a small and discreet warehouse just off Smith Street in Collingwood that was actively accepting and distributing a range of products to various locations. Although the significance had been missed, it was likely that a recent shipment of church organ pipes from Belgium had quantities of methamphetamines hidden inside them, and cocaine buried in their fibre. Linda reflected that the inventiveness within the crooks' world was endless.

Slowly evolving for Linda and her team and coming to light was the evidence that they were in fact dealing with two separate gang identities that overlapped through the personalities involved brushing up together.

The first gang, a sex slavery group, was controlled by Freda Zellerman who received instructions through Sam Hoggard, who was the communicator/local operator for an Asian cartel based in Thailand. The cartel members were inhumane and ruthless, and did not value their human 'products' at all, or often their members either.

Linda realised that Freda was not a very sophisticated crook, but carried out instructions given to her. Freda was used to controlling prostitutes, parties, pornography, organising events, and making sure the logistics were taken care of. That included ensuring that food, facilities, alcohol and recreational drugs were comfortably available. She fraternised with all and sundry, ranging from pillars of society to bikie gangs. She worked with suppliers but was not the origin of the products. Freda was considered efficient, reliable and tough and provided a good show. She certainly had the right connections. Project Manager and even Fixer.

Linda reflected that probably Freda's main motivators at this time in her life were the thrill, the money, ego, fear, and maybe some evil. Freda guided and motivated the actions of new and desperate fledgling criminals involved in unsophisticated robberies and burglaries, and even fenced for them, moving on valuable jewellery and diamonds to a different level.

She enjoyed promoting the social gatherings such as those on the luxury yacht at Williamstown as 'Fun for the Daring and Discerning' or even perhaps the 'Brave and Confident'. They attracted Reggie McGuiness and some of his cronies. Freda had an absolute hatred for those who she referred to as snitches, infos, and rats. She made it clear to employees the retaliation to expect for leaking. She had a formidable way with explanations.

The other gang, a drug and serious crime group, was different and much more deeply buried. This was the John Silverman group, and it was in a different league. Unofficially this group was part of an international crime syndicate. What they actually controlled in Melbourne was not known by police at this stage. Linda summarised to her team that a short list could include large amounts of cash, money laundering, importing and wholesaling of drugs, liaising activities with other major crime groups.

many years, a greatly under-recognised senior criminal in Victoria. His pleasant and low-key façade made him appear as not much more than a fringe player in the lower levels of criminal activities and no major threat to man or beast. He had no obvious or regular contact with John Silverman.

35

Ricky Russo and Freda Zellerman

It was of great interest to the police team to see the apparent close personal relationship now between Ricky Russo and Freda Zellerman. It was obvious that they were trying to minimise their visible time together to hide any evidence of an unofficial alliance. On the surface it was a most unlikely coupling. Linda thought that no matchmaking company would have ever introduced them, even given that opposites attract!

Freda was, 'What you see is what you get!' She had a really fit body as a result of regular gym work and she was often seen in colourful, skin-tight lycra gear. What astounded most witnesses were the tattoos covering all the visible areas of her body — including on her neck and right up under her chin. To add emphasis, she used heavy black mascara and large false eyelashes. She had face rings of many sizes and shapes, in eyebrows and nostrils, and her lips were as described as 'pouty duck lips'.

Freda was a talkative and friend

comfortable in nightclubs or general music venues, and even at a pole dancing club. She was certainly very different and could not be missed. The fact that she had been spotted in Williamstown pushing a pram with a pet dog in it described her attitude. Freda had experienced the tough side of humanity.

Ricky Russo was a criminal from a softer side. He had charm, good looks, and really was not a vicious person. That did not mean he had never commissioned violence to achieve an end, however. As a young man he had had his uncle Paul Wheeler watching over him, and positioning him into places of strength without over-exposing him to the police. His name was affixed to many documents from which he could benefit, but not to any that could attach criminal responsibility to him.

It was known that Ricky was active in minor criminality but his quiet and shy demeanour meant he was mainly underestimated in the world of serious or heavy crime. The music venues and nightclubs were very comfortable for him as his low profile allowed him to hide. He was a charming man to meet and he had style.

Linda thought what strange bedfellows they seemed. But their similar criminalities had brought them together.

It may have seemed OK for Freda and Helen Murphy to go shopping and to be having coffee and cakes together, but it would have been unlikely for Freda and Ricky to parade in the streets together. Freda had her own apartment in Russell Street, so that had been the site of their first genuine rendezvous. It had been arranged at short notice after a few drinks in the Lounge of the Sofitel Melbourne on Collins Street, where gaping upmarket patrons had made them feel uncomfortable. It was not even a mutually attractive progression. Rather a pent-up sexual desire that needed satisfying.

They were known to each other, as their activities had often coincided, as had the underage sex trafficking on the yacht in Williamstown. Although not in the same team (or league), with instructions coming from different bases — Sam Hoggard to Freda and John Silverman to Ricky — they were clearly not antagonistic rivals. Some form of fraternising was inevitable.

The visit to the Russell Street apartment was for Ricky full of curiosity and expectation. In his own quiet way, he was buzzing with anticipation. In his mind there was no doubt that Freda would be a sex expert. It was her 'business'. Much more than that, he was curious to see her wonderfully tuned physique fully exposed and to see just how much of her body was covered with tattoos.

He knew her personality was loud and vibrant and in keeping with her bold appearance and he expected a lot. Ricky was not disappointed as all clothing was quickly disposed of to reveal almost every part of Freda decorated with 'body art' — even where a Brazilian wax had been executed. Freda expertly demonstrated how a well-tuned body could contort into unlikely positions that seemed to Ricky to almost defy gravity.

Ricky had no problem following the in-skin artwork that in some illustrations pointed him to the intimate locker door. He chased with his lips and tongue and was quite sure he had never ever experienced anything like it before. It was huge fun for both of them. Freda was as he had anticipated: noisy, energetic and vigorous. Expert was the word that came to Ricky's mind. There had been no suggestion that this was about love. It was pure sex, to be enjoyed with abandon.

Freda had a different emotion. From her very early days, she had been exposed to and forced into actions and relationships that were not always pleasant, or even of her own volition, and were often entered into simply for her to obtain a benefit. She was now old enough and powerful enough to indulge in sex only when and if she wanted to or felt the need. That was not very often now, because she preferred to also like her chosen partner.

This coupling was a success. Ricky was calm, gentle and respectful. He was obviously fascinated by her persona and appearance, and he had the stamina and enthusiasm to prolong the physical activity. He did not resent her suggesting actions and positions that he clearly had not previously experienced. They had harmony on the occasion. This was not an occasion to be exchanging confidential data and no efforts were made in that direction. Ricky stayed the night content in the comfort offered and they found out that they liked each other. A simple coffee and toast together in the morning concluded a pleasant interlude for both. They both told each other how good it had been and agreed to future meetings.

36
Quandary

Ricky Russo was in a small quandary. What exactly was Helen Murphy expected to provide — and to whom? Linda Alexander and her OCS team were in a similar quandary, wondering how Helen Murphy would add to or detract from their quest to solve the several crimes on which they were working.

Ricky clearly knew his role in the greater picture. He was the deeply planted and trusted member of the UK international crime syndicate. His role was to appear low key and almost ineffectual. The syndicate was part of a huge money laundering operation dealing with massive amounts of monies generated from crime in many countries. They were also involved in the drug trade all over the world, with members being serious criminals determined to remain anonymous. They were ruthless.

Freda was in a different category. Her criminal involvement was controlled by crooked solicitor Sam Hoggard, who passed on to her instructions for activities and responsibilities. She was not overendowed with a high IQ. She knew how to organise at ubs, the entertainment and functions for the various 'high rollers' who enjoyed a good time there. Low-level drug use and smuggling things of low value she could arrange. Prostitution and slavery were also within her capabilities. Freda could resort to violence or arrange it if necessary, and she had connections with some bikie gangs, but she was not an expert trading in gold or diamonds, antiques or manuscripts.

The Police Commissioner had recently decreed that the police force was to investigate opportunities for good public relations opportunities. This came into being when a raid on Crown Casino in Southbank became a top plan. It was a combined action including the OCS, support from regular Melbourne officers and the Federal Police. The new term 'Multi-Agency Task Force' was the latest phrase on everyone's lips.

The midnight raid on the casino went well, with uniformed and plainclothes detectives, several police vehicles parked in full view by the foyer, and a conspicuous blue-grey bus at the ready. They targeted illegals, bail skippers, known criminals, gamblers with no identities, two known drug dealers and staff with false identities, and these were all rounded up into either the bus or other police vehicles. Several bikie patrons acted up tough so they were also arrested and taken away. Police PR officers had done their tip-offs well, so media representatives from major print and TV outlets were there as witnesses.

Several quality pictures were taken that all featured Linda prominently and she was identified as the senior officer of the evening. As usual, over-emphasised by the press — the raid was labelled a "major crackdown on drugs and money laundering".

Within the police force it was considered a great success,

and along with her associates and peers, Linda copped lots of good-humoured banter. They called her a superstar and 'Ms Hollywood' while acknowledging she really had done a great job. Linda felt she had come a long way from her early Western Australian police days, where one angry police associate had labelled her "pompous twit".

Perhaps her current confidence coincided with a change in her personal life. Always close to her brother Brendan, with whom she shared an apartment, she now considered she really owed him big time for all his support. The home they shared was always immaculate as they employed a regular cleaner and they were both clean and tidy people. Visitors were easy to accommodate. Linda had been with her partner Jeremy for many years, but it had slipped into an easy routine of sameness and they had never lived together.

The change that occurred came from within Brendan's workplace — a large commercial enterprise. He had introduced one of his current senior associates, Hugh, to Linda. Without the usual tedious formal introductions or a protracted 'getting to know you' period, they had immediately become attracted. They dated a few times and then for reasonable privacy the town of Daylesford became a favourite of them both. The town was full of interest as they wandered and explored old hotels, orchards, hot springs, and best of all the Lake House. Both were now in their mid-thirties, mature in relationships but they found themselves deeply attracted to each other, like young lovers.

One of the early points of pleasure occurred as they were walking in the main street of Daylesford. Linda had staggere slightly over a kerb and Hugh had automatically put his arm out to steady her and then circled his arm around her waist. Linda felt the electricity sizzle, and the heat rise within both her and Hugh. They walked on in silence as they both enjoyed the erotic feelings and the simplicity of it all.

For the first time ever, it occurred to Linda that her biological clock was running along, and she rang her friend Beth Jenkins, still based at Woodend, just to chat and tell her of her latest news. Beth was excited for her and suggested coffee or a meal in Woodend could be good. Beth's advice to Linda was, "Go for it!" With quite a bit of excitement, Linda decided to book the Lake House in Daylesford for two nights, even though they could only spend the Saturday night there. Linda confessed to Hugh that she had a long-time companion, but he was quick to reply, "yes, OK, but didn't you indicate it was really over and mainly platonic now?"

Linda found it quite hard to admit that was so, for many reasons; mainly feelings of guilt. But most of the reasons of comfort and loyalty went out the window as soon as the unit door had closed and Hugh kissed her first with gentleness, and then with deep passion. She felt his hand inside her blouse and she caught her breath. The kiss deepened and her skin was crying out to be massaged. Linda almost wanted to confess to him that she had had sex with only one man in the past four years, and a grand total of less than the fingers on one hand, so please be gentle! She could hardly catch her breath as the intensity increased to the first stage of a wonderful experience of exotic sex.

37

John Silverman

The OCS was continuing to beaver away into every nook and cranny imaginable, closing in on their list of potential crime figures. Attention was concentrated on John Silverman. Or should it be Reggie McGuiness? There was no doubt that someone involved had great nimbleness of body and mind that enabled them to be a step ahead. They moved the goal posts and more importantly they kept moving stock.

Linda, Ian, and all other staff at various times, over many coffees and other stimulants, spent many hours discussing and examining the current situation. Happily, their office facilities and morale allowed them to be comfortable with long and tedious repetitions. They knew there had to be a weak link in the chain somewhere, and quietly Linda and Ian settled on their unanimous choice of Ricky Russo. It was apparent he had some relationship in both 'camps. They quite rightly concluded that John Silverman was a different kettle of fish, but they decided as a first step to rattle the cage that seemed to protect him.

An interview was arranged under the guise of inquiries about promotions, connections and media activities that were common areas of activity for his 'boss' Reggie McGuiness. Some of these took place on premises of doubtful integrity and could be seen to be useful for money laundering. John Silverman, in the interview, virtually scoffed at the idea of any money laundering, even though it was presented in the mildest fashion. Linda however, thought she had seen a flash of bleakness in his expression before a quick reversion to his usual smoothness. Other questions about ownership of premises in and around Russell and Exhibition Streets in Melbourne met with bland looks and no eye flicker at all. A question about a wholesale warehouse in Kororoit Creek Road in Williamstown received the same reaction. His response to both questions was just a negative. The interview was short and unfriendly as anticipated, but was intended to convey a message.

A few weeks later, Linda and Ian put into action the main part of their unorthodox plan by virtually kidnapping Ricky Russo as he walked alone in broad daylight in Little Flinders Street in the City. They had previously plotted his usual daily habit in the narrow one-way street close to Spring Street, and this time saw him walking to the car park to retrieve his car. In a plain Holden they pulled up beside him, opened the back door and 'insisted' he join them. Some strong verbal persuasion was needed. Once he was in, with urgency, the police car raced into Exhibition Street and across town to premises that held several empty offices that were used on occasion for private discussions. No one in the public reported untoward behaviour, so no explanations were needed. Russo was introduced to several police officers known as 'special agents', holding an off-the-record interview specially to seek cooperation and to inform him of his status. They suggested it would take no more than thirty minutes. It was as relaxed as it could be, and with another assurance that this was an off-the-record meeting, all attempting to give Russo a 'heads up' as to give him a fair go.

Ricky did not misunderstand the significance and did as he was told: "Sit there and listen."

In gentle and polite terms, they summarised his position. Going back a long way they reminded him he had been a small-time drug runner and had at times helped to identify crooks moving into his or his boss's territory. He clearly had matured and was rewarded by his peers with an expansion of his territories and seniority. Financial rewards increased significantly and Ricky had had the intelligence or guidance to treat the rewards with care and consideration. Silence followed this summary.

Linda spoke to Ricky; "Firstly, we respect that you are an excellent competition table tennis player, and you regularly play bridge both online and at your club." This intimate knowledge was given with a genuine look of respect from both the officers.

"Secondly, we know how well you have respected and protected your ill-gotten gains." Ricky just looked at Inspector McDonald with an element of smugness that probably said, 'you don't know anything'.

Ian then listed for him, reading from a set of notes, his assets. "Let's start with family assets; Subaru cars, family homes for parents and cousins, share portfolios, shell companies and trusts in Australia, and those mystery accounts in Samoa, Vanuatu, and Cayman Islands."

In a light-hearted aside Linda added, "We are not yet sure about Guernsey!"

Now they had his attention, and without yet saying anything about Freda Zellerman or the two Filipina women. The main purpose of the interview was to move on to concentrate on John Silverman. Now they certainly had his attention.

In the softest possible manner and in low voices, they informed him he was in deep trouble from which there was no exit. Ricky was an experienced mature criminal and it took him only a few minutes to realise that he was in 'deep shit'. It was almost unnecessary but Linda reminded him, "This is the end of the road for your current activities and you no doubt know that gaol is almost certain, and all your assets will be frozen. Think of the effect on your family and friends."

That did not take long to sink in, and Ricky was a nimble thinker.

Ian McDonald added, "You must know your mate Sam Hoggard is also under investigation and details are flowing forth from him."

That seemed a little surprising and Ricky was quick to respond, "Of course I know him but I take no instructions from him."

Smoothly Ian added, "Oh yes, we knew that, as he gives instructions to your partner, Freda."

That created agitation, and Ricky went into an explanation

of the 'true' relationship with Freda Zellerman. This took time, and the officers informed him they had plenty of time to devote to him and his information. At this stage all was still off the record and confidential. They emphasised he was being given a 'break' but with only a tiny chance. They alluded to re-establishment and a new personality, out of state or even offshore. All in vague utterances with no promises. Then came the crunch questions regarding Silverman.

Linda started off with, "We find John Silverman an enigma. He has us puzzled. He is so private and mysterious. What we do know is he is a crook. Now, we will tell you what we know about him. He hides under his association with Reggie McGuiness. He has his own tightly confidential office in Lygon Street, from where he sends encrypted messages all over the world. It appears he owns or controls premises in Collingwood and in Kororoit Creek Road in Altona, used for general warehouse purposes."

Ricky put on a 'far-away' face as if he was hearing rubbish.

Linda said, "He does use a little old not-so-innocent runner to relay messages and he works out of Bishop Court in Clarendon Street, East Melbourne."

Linda stressed that it was a very sophisticated operation. She added in a low voice, "Dance with the devil and reap the consequences. What we also know is that you report to John Silverman."

38

Silverman / Russo

The meeting continued for over an hour as the police officers laid on the line all the consequences of the information they were sharing. Ricky Russo was clearly aware of the message being given and at one point murmured, "I'm a dead man!"

Ian unsympathetically said, "I think I agree."

Linda reflected to herself that it was looking more and more if this was the chink in the armour they had been seeking.

What type of mutually beneficial actions could be contemplated? That was the real question. What did either side have to trade? Russo was blindingly aware that his predicament was dire. Very wisely he sat, fidgeted, looked at the floor, the walls and the ceiling, as he waited for suggestions to evolve.

Within the vagaries that the subject had previously presented was now a glimpse of light. The two detectives highlighted that it could be that punishment for some offences could be traded or offset by contributions in a different arena. Ricky looked up but was not aggressive enough to ask what the hell that meant.

A clear indication was given by Linda that she wanted full answers to some simple questions before any forward progress could be made. Being in no position to negotiate, Ricky simply nodded his head in agreement.

Linda and Ian outlined five simple requirements, stressing that any leaking of their meeting or subjects discussed would be denied and disclosure would follow, as would arrests. They told Russo there would be two full days before they were all to meet up again, and nothing would be put in writing or recorded in any fashion.

Ian stressed, "This will be your one and only chance to disappear and be safe. If you do not cooperate, we will pull you off the street without warning!"

The list of items included all phone numbers used to contact John Silverman and UK contacts, their full names if known, any known criminal connections with Reggie McGuiness and Tony Matheson. A full list of properties owned or controlled by Silverman or nominees, e.g. a warehouse and residence in Creswick or Geelong? Also, a list of employees from the Collingwood premises. Bikie gang networks and distributions. Sam Hoggard and Randle and Randle connections.

Because no written list was generated, it was agreed that if Ricky could not remember all details in full, part answers or additional information would be OK and understood. Then they unceremoniously they packed him back into the rear seat of the dark blue Holden Commodore and dropped him off in Exhibition Street.

Snippets of information they had gath

included that the fling he had had with Freda Zellerman was over, and he understood the criminal label he could attract as being guilty by association. A leading remark had been made about Helen Murphy but no comment came from Ricky.

As an indication of compliance with the police demands, Ricky's first contribution was that some properties in Creswick would be worth examining. They were both residential and commercial, and were probably listed as owned by Johan Sebastian Silverman. Creswick was less than twenty kilometres from Ballarat and had a population of under five thousand.

Quiet and confidential police inquiries revealed at least three properties owned by a J Silverman, with two of them protected by council heritage overlays. A substantial and well-maintained four-bedroom Edwardian home with broad verandas in Mason Street, Creswick, was of interest. It was occupied by an elderly, semi-retired man and his wife, however further inquiries established regular amounts of mail addressed to him were delivered, as was other mail to other names, from banks, brokers and insurance agents.

Mr Guy Rackham, ex-con and on a pension, maintained the property in immaculate condition. He also held the keys for a well-maintained warehouse a short distance away. The police established there were no records of properties owned by Guy Rackham or his wife, and they assumed he was being generously looked after. It was not possible to have a look inside the secure and protected commercial building without arousing suspicion, but police continued to dig deeply into the background associations and family.

39
Helen Murphy

Freda Zellerman was doing a thorough job of initiating a willing pupil into the group in Helen Murphy. They were completely different personalities; there was not much subterfuge about Freda, and the aspects of her personality she did try to moderate or hide were not that subtle or clever. This was in real contrast to Helen, who was a presentation in deception. A 'friendship' of convenience to both.

Interestingly, their socialising had apparently gradually been modified too; now being together only at night. They had separate apartments but matched transport and events to be together. Many appearances were at nightclubs and musical events across the city and they mixed with all levels of patrons.

Freda regularly delivered information to her sources and drugs to serious associates. It had become obvious to Helen that Freda had close associations with at least one of the major bikie groups. Pick-up and delivery of products was done in the most street fashion, for which large amounts of cash (only) were exchanged. Where that cash was disposed of was well hidden from Helen. The two women drank and laughed together but there were no close emotional bonds. They had plenty of money to spend so could indulge themselves at will. They did not frequent top-end restaurants because their appearance caused too many comments, even as Freda enjoyed the limelight and the notoriety.

In comparison, social life and enjoyment had leapt forward for Linda Alexander. Her new boyfriend, Hugh Moorcraft, was becoming an unexpected serious romance. They had a serious sexual relationship by now, and also found time to enjoy meals together. Apart from Daylesford, another favourite place when they could manage it was a top end, expensive modern Chinese restaurant in Melbourne. The beautiful, stylish interior and relaxed culture suited the growing relationship with all of its pressures. However, often it was better to just grab a kerbside pickup as time became the most important factor. When they were both available, they enjoyed the modern Chinese food and friendly staff.

When there was no time pressure, they huddled together to build their closeness, and Linda vividly remembered the first time when Hugh — over a glass of red wine — looked deeply into her eyes and said, "Thank you just for being you!"

It was very tender and meaningful. She bent over to kiss him gently on the mouth and responded, "How have we advanced so far so quickly?"

It was later that Linda felt a pang of guilt, or was it reality, as she reflected on a sense of wonderment about how he could be so attracted to the intriguing and fascinating Inspector Linda Alexander!

What a time of pleasure for them both, wandering down a deep emotional road not travelled before by either of them. When would they be brave enough to introduce one another to parents? They were still getting to know one another and to enjoy favourite things together.

They had discovered a mutual joy in listening to a little-known Aussie balladeer called Kevin Johnson. For Linda it was two old songs, 'Bonnie Please Don't Go' — which made her very sad about South Africa — and the more widely acclaimed 'Rock and Roll; I gave you the best years of my life' that were her favourites. Seemed like the life story for many people, she thought. It was all about great fun and enjoyment together as their appreciation of common interests grew.

40
Russo Feedback

Linda Alexander and Ian McDonald felt certain they were on the cusp of solving two crime scenarios, if they could just crack the Ricky Russo façade. At what cost to him, and how to offer an offset? In just under two days from the initial 'capture' meeting, he made tentative contact with them through a known friendly constable to pass on a message: 'Jack says OK'.

Russo was then surreptitiously picked up and taken to a secure location for interrogation. Less than a full day was assigned to this questioning which was designed to be harmonious, with no threats of tough police action. The emphasis was to be on a 'quid pro quo' of confidential and valuable information exchange, with a guaranteed safety exit for him.

Ricky volunteered simple answers to most of the points he had previously been given, and a new set of refined questions were provided. He stressed repeatedly the total confidentiality needed. "My life depends on that!" Ricky said.

He had begun to appreciate he had nowhere else to go.

The meeting concluded, and armed with the new information the police team dispersed with an assurance they would meet again soon. Linda and Ian immediately convened a top-level police conference for authorisation to commence actions.

One of the first activities arranged was for a uniformed senior sergeant to make a 'routine' call on the premises of the warehouse in Collingwood, which was thought to be on occasions no more than a convenient stepping stone for illicit drugs. The visit was nothing more than a routine call over a minor bylaw complaint about unregistered loaders on the street. The manager agreed he was also the stock controller and seemed mystified by the visit. He thought a complaint seemed unfair, and added he had been an employee for over five years. Warehouse products covered a wide range but were mainly for CBD retailers.

The manager was happy to show the sergeant around and in chatting informally offered that he had health problems and he felt life was unfair: "I have lived all my life very cautiously, and now at the age of sixty-two poor health has ambushed me!" he complained. "I have never been a smoker and alcoholic drinks have not touched my lips! How come?"

Reporting back to the police team, the sergeant's judgement was that the manager was not a criminal; he was unlikely to be more than a reliable, not too bright employee who simply moved stock on, as ordered by superiors.

Progress with other information from Russo was much more cautious and circumspect. Huge potential results were riding on total accuracy and integrity. Linda a██████ r almost living in the office as they tracked down every lead and possibility. The list of possessions and properties owned or directly controlled by John Silverman grew to an alarming level. Pleasing, however, was that most of the high-profile people with whom he mixed were clearly innocent bystanders.

The most active property seemed to be the warehouse and office complex in Kororoit Creek Road, Altona. It was owned by a shell company which was owned by a trust, with the registered address being the office of a city group of solicitors. All appeared to be normal with tax returns and company details. An around-the-clock police watch was instigated.

Linda racked her brains on how else to drag up information in other areas of the state without alarming the local constabulary or prompting curious leaks from within the associated teams. Linda had done well in the Goldfields region and Macedon Ranges in previous cases, so she rang Beth Jenkins to arrange a coffee meeting in Woodend.

Turning first to the personal, Linda gave an update on her situation with boyfriend Hugh, and Beth gave an update on her marriage. Both women were travelling well. On the more pressing reason for the meeting, Beth suggested a phone call or visit to Bria Moretti and Cliff Richardson — now long-term partners in both life and business and whom Linda and Beth had met through a previous case — could be worthwhile for Linda because of their background and involvement in properties, community and businesses in Geelong, Creswick and Ballarat. Without hesitation, Linda telephoned Bria Moretti at the successful retail and wholesale bicycle business in Ballarat, and invited herself and deputy Inspector Ian McDonald for an-off-the record visit.

As hoped, when the meeting took place, Bria greeted her warmly and said she and Cliff were delighted to catch up. It was just the type of greeting Linda had hoped for. They were all relaxed by the inclusion of Ian McDonald. After the usual preliminaries, Linda explained what a long bow they were pursuing and, with a rider that there were 'no alarm bells ringing' necessarily in the activities, she asked if they could help in a little sleuthing about property ownerships and specific activities in the central Victorian Goldfields' local areas.

No problems at all, was the response; in fact, Bria and Cliff were delighted to be of any assistance. The properties were listed out for them, as was a request for any unusual behaviour or vehicle movements. The informal discussions wandered on for two hours before Linda and Ian made their excuses and left.

On the way back into the city Linda reminisced in general to Ian, saying how enjoyable it was to be meeting and talking in open terms with those with whom you have much in common. They both agreed how good it was to be with close companions, as being a police officer had its down sides.

Back in the police station, new information was constantly being analysed and dissected and very quickly new details flowed in from the Goldfields. In particular, much more about the Creswick 'caretaker'. He seemed like a potential informer, Linda thought. Where to look and why? What information would or could be stored in the beautiful Edwardian house in Mason Street in Creswick?

Checking the veracity of information that flowed in was not difficult with the resources available to the police. The caretaker, Guy Rackham, was quickly identified as hailing from Adelaide, where previously over many years he had been employed as a vicious enforcer for a drug cartel, but ill health and peer pressure had finally contributed to his 'retirement'. It was hard to believe such an attractive-looking elderly man could have such a past. Creswick seemed a good town to retire in and had attractive legitimate community organisations — such as the Seed Bank, a not-for-profit group — doing great things. Many Creswick residents were happy, contented volunteers.

Further inquiries elicited the information that his oldest son was quite the 'gun' still in Adelaide drug circles. Rackham senior was moved well up the list for potential incarceration.

From the 'Ricky list' of suspect properties came a new one that seemed worthy of physical investigation with a low likelihood of raising alarm. A battered old wool store in Clunes close to the Mechanics Institute building had a mystery ownership. This would require clandestine entry as it was vital that they not alert the owner or occupier of their interest. Was the building, or the contents, security alarmed?

It was not difficult for Linda to have the task duly authorised, and the results of an entry through the ceiling appeared via a classified email within days. Covered with tarpaulins and undisturbed dust in the wool store was quite a fortune; three classic and vintage Rolls Royce cars, an E-Type Jaguar, original paintings, lock boxes, and a formidable large safe. The premises were left unmarked by the covert entry.

All the information being accrued was being tested and verified. Linda and Ian and the team at OCS were becoming more excited about the discoveries.

41

The Team: Hoggard, Freda, Helen

To whom did Sam Hoggard report? The police Interceptions team concluded it was to a contact in the UK. Freda had been supplied from the same UK group to strengthen the local small crime group operating sex slavery in Australia. Ricky Russo had become a low-level social associate with useful connections. Hoggard was seen as an incompetent and lazy group head, and was not in charge of a large crime group. Drugs, entertainment and fencing stolen goods for bikies and young immigrant gangs were the main sources of income. Through Hoggard, properties were set up in trusts and shell companies that hid true ownerships and control. Randle and Randle, Lawyers, were a mainstream firm of good reputation and as such they were well informed of future and major events in Melbourne. Sam Hoggard as a middle manager did only as much as he had to to continue to work there.

A major event on Melbourne's calendar was an annual Bike Show held in and around the Exhibition Centre on Nicholson

Street and Carlton Gardens in the CBD. It was a big event with local radio and some TV coverage, so naturally Reggie McGuiness was involved in the planning and preparation, as well as participation in the event. Public relations around such a show was both public and private to achieve maximum exposure.

The motor bike brands ranged from small, new and little-known names from unlikely sources, to the very large and popular names, some of which were distributed by one controlling local wholesaler. Marketing for such an event depends on 'who you know' and the size of your budget. Reggie McGuiness was seen as knowing the ropes and people who could be potential buyers.

Word filtered down to event organisers that an exclusive, invitation-only event coinciding with the major show evening would be welcome, and appropriate. It would be quite a balancing act considering the wide range of attendees; from Indian and Harley motorbike types to the less reputable with more money than they could use, but with little or no respect for law and order. What would be an appropriate dress code?

A team was assembled to organise a marquee on a suitable site, as planning got underway. A highly skilled event management company was appointed. Sam Hoggard was able to insist that Helen Murphy be included in the planning for security duties because of her police background. Freda — even in cover up clothing mode — would not be included. That did not matter as she was a key unofficial product supplier.

Serious logistics needed to be considered. A fun party along the lines of the Williamstown yacht event? Or a combined fun and frolic for the more 'respectable'? Or strictly invite-only at specific times? Also, an unofficial distribution centre would be required for those pre-approved other regular customers. Risky, but Freda decided to consult her major supplier at Kororoit Creek Road for a list of availability and prices. The basics she nominated for pickup in a little over a month included methamphetamines, marijuana, MDMA, plus 'adequate' amounts of cocaine. She knew her way around well enough to enquire about additions and variations. With tacit approval and support of Reggie McGuiness and his associates, the event preparations rolled on.

With an intuitive impulse that was becoming valuable, Linda, after becoming aware of the event and with police informers advising of possible drug interest, picked up the phone and called Cliff Richardson, who lived in Geelong. She first asked whether he or Bria had discovered any new information about the property in Mason Street, Creswick. Cliff admitted little progress except that the property was known to be exceptionally well maintained. Linda then also slipped in an extra wish about a property in Clunes which Cliff offered to have a look at. She then went on to her main reason for calling, "Cliff, this is a high-level request for your help. You may know about the annual Motorbike Show that takes place in the Exhibition Centre in Melbourne?"

He replied, "Yes, sort of, but we are not directly involved."

Linda said, "Well, here is the favour we want, please." She went on to explain and ask for his company to apply to participate in the show, anticipating a negative response, but outlining the strong basis for their Ballarat Super Bike Shop to be included because of the electrification of many of their models. Cliff was to push for inclusion and to offer large marketing contributions. It would probably require Cliff and Bria to personally visit the CEO of the show or even Reggie McGuiness. Cliff really liked the idea and was enthusiastic and optimistic that they could be included. He felt it was a genuine cause to pursue on behalf of their modern business enterprise.

Linda explained that there may be some unusual offers of participation to take note of, and that any invitations to attend event functions could be useful, i.e. fringe inclusions such as luxury car franchising, or BMW bikes, or cars as incentives.

That impulse had gone well for Linda, and another she now had — and more often than she would admit to — was to call Hugh just to say, "Hello, how are you?"

No one was keeping count but it was obvious the habit was growing into more than once a day, even though they both had tight timetables. They found they had worked into a list of favourite songs and singers just of their own. Apart from Kevin Johnson and his limited popular titles they now also embraced a huge range of much more emotional songs, notably by Anne Murray and Judy Collins.

Back on the work front, a team of specialist officers was studying the information flowing daily from Ricky Russo. Analysts were seconded to the OCS team to speed up checking the accuracy of information and to help on the timing and detail to enact any arrests. There was concern over the possibility of

Ricky breaking down and exposing information to the wrong people, perhaps through his realising the magnitude of his actions and the probable outcome.

A decision was made to shorten the time he could be at large to protect him and the information being supplied. Superintendent Brunton was consulted and he urged haste as he had seen too many potential hits blown out of the water by leaks and delays. He rightly identified the danger of Sam Hoggard somehow becoming aware of danger signals, so a plan was devised to totally distract him from any local inquisition.

A small break-in was arranged at the premises of Randle and Randle, Lawyers, with the apparent intent to steal and/or damage electronic equipment and when that failed, in frustration the thieves smashed and damaged offices, including random distribution of filth. Significant areas of office space were damaged, including that occupied by Sam Hoggard, which was a huge distraction for him.

The major requirement for Hoggard was a time and date for the pickup of the massive quantity of drugs ordered by Freda for use in and around the Bike Show. The usual terms of payment were reiterated, i.e. fifty percent cash up front and the balance on pickup. This was more than tens of thousands of dollars, but ready cash that Hoggard could supply. All was proceeding smoothly.

42

Ricky Russo

Ricky was abundantly clear in his own mind that he was now well down a one-way road from which there was little or no option to reverse. It really focused his mind and thinking to recall his early upbringing and the part his friends and family had played. When considering his mother, he liked the ode written by a man on a train that said, "I rose and gave her my seat — I could not let her stand, she made me think of Mother, with that strap held in her hand."

His schooling had been religious, but Ricky had progressed into being agnostic — not quite an atheist. He had enjoyed school, going through with humour and a liking for worthwhile quotes, which he often used to break a silence. Perhaps some of those attributes had smoothed his entry into low-level crime. A favourite quote of his was, "Deception. Half the work that is done in this world is to make things appear to be what they are not." — ER Beadle. Ricky also often quoted quietly to himself, "If I should die think only this of me," and a significant later line, "And think this heart, all evil shed away, a pulse in the eternal mind, no less," from a famous poem by Rupert Brooke written in 1915.

Feeling not quite morose but contemplative, Ricky tried to summarise his own position to himself, as he was fully aware that by simply disappearing, it was unlikely any other tributes would be given about him. His first decision was to record what was to be included in his will. No wider family; no children, uncles, aunties or cousins or any family other than his mother and father — of whom he was very fond. A major sum was specified to the Royal Flying Doctor Service of Australia. Even though he did not own a dog, an amount was to be set aside for a regular contribution over five years to the Lost Dogs Home and RSPCA, Melbourne. It showed a slightly quirky sense of humour, and he hoped his Mum and Dad would be proud of him.

Ricky was a little ashamed because he prided himself on optimistic thinking, but he wanted to be respected as a gentleman who could hold a confidence and be respected for integrity. He knew his behaviour had pushed the limits but he also felt he had earned his reputation for being a quiet, solid associate over a long period. Knowing the end may be near to his current status concentrated the mind.

Ricky had read a wonderful book called 'Tuesdays with Morrie' by Mitch Albom, and although he had read it many years previously, its insights had never faded and it gave him new thoughts for consideration. He wished to be remembered as a good man, not a bad man.

All along the way, Linda was liaising closely and secretly with Ricky. In a strange way, they became professional friends, as they had crossed paths as far back as the 'Twin Bins' case involving Gussie the necrophiliac. Linda had found him a decent man then, and still did. She had to keep reassuring him that the police would and were currently protecting him. He was not so confident, and kept trying to bury his morbid thoughts.

Hoggard was distracted by the break-in at R&R Lawyers premises, but instinct and intuition warned him that something else was going on, and he renewed his questions to Freda and Helen, who he now regarded as part of the team.

The Bike Show was the current big news and everyone was excited about such a major event. Unusually for him, Sam Hoggard called for a highly confidential, in-person meeting for the three of them. It was held in the back room of a coffee shop close to the Victoria Markets where someone well tattooed would not cause much interest.

The agenda was to discuss in detail all the activities planned in association with the Bike Show. Freda reported she was liaising closely with John Grey, a deputy of Reggie McGuiness, to operate the marquee and associated activities over the Bike Show weekend. Sam indicated he was experiencing pressure from his associates to take advantage of the circumstances surrounding such an event. He gave examples including the presence of big-spending club members who spent outside normal constraints.

The women indicated awareness of this and were including sex workers of various types for the more particular 'high-fliers'. Food, alcohol and recreational drugs were all on order. Sam did not enquire about their sources as he considered that was not his territory or expertise.

Other organisations were anticipating a big-spending event. The need for financial care and secure methods of payment were discussed. An indication of budget constraints was given. Sam stressed the need for total anonymity as there seemed to be some unusual activity in the Australian Federal Police that his sources were identifying. He stressed again he was not to be directly communicated with. A short Q&A session concluded the meeting, which had apparently not been witnessed.

43

John Silverman

A Bike Show, a footy final, a Grand Prix, a Melbourne Cup, or any major collection of people with money to spend was of interest. Most such major events made contact with Reggie McGuiness, so JS Silverman company was alerted.

Criminals were on the fringe of all activities. Strong criminal groups were aware of their competitors and the sensible ones tried not to be competitive by sticking to their knitting. John Silverman had kept his activities to a narrow range that suited his well-disguised control area and his powerful overseas associates. Silverman considered his turf was top-end bulk drugs, serious money laundering, top-level hostess services, high-value art and documents, and anonymous property investments. He was determined to remain low profile, and he could activate physical persuasion when required.

Silverman was a high-level international crime associate who was expert in maintaining personal and corporate security around himself. Ricky Russo was a minor part of his team but

John had always kept him at arm's length, keeping him away from any details of his modus operandi. Reggie McGuiness was also a very useful cover for his more nefarious activities. Silverman was aware of the activities of Sam Hoggard, but it was probable that Hoggard was not aware of Silverman.

44
The Pick Up

With the fifty percent cash payment completed for the Bike Show event, the address, date and time for completion of the drug transaction had been agreed: a Thursday night, 1.30am at the premises on Kororoit Creek Road, Altona — with entry only through the back, unlit, single door. Nothing recorded but details well understood. Two only recipients to be involved, and to use agreed passwords.

The date, time and location of a huge and valuable consignment was whispered about and rumours filtered through to Ricky Russo. Ricky realised this information was his exit, so he contacted Linda for an official meeting with important information.

Chief Ron Brunton attended, firstly extending his thanks, and then outlining the necessary steps to resettle Ricky, probably in New Zealand, to be immediately put into motion. The date for him to 'disappear' was agreed.

A request for a search warrant for the Altona premises was

instigated and Linda and Ian swung into action preparing the team for the raid. They delayed notifying the AFP until closer to the date for security reasons. The plan in detail, including all lines of communication and authority, was noted. The need for absolute confidentiality was again foremost in all communications as excitement and expectations continued to rise. The level of anticipation within the OCS team and police command was extraordinary.

In the premises at Kororoit Creek Road, the level of excitement and anticipation was also high. The Boss was supervising his two staff members as they selected and packed the large order. They did not know or care who the order was for, but were aware of the significance and the value of an order this big. The packed goods had to be available by 5pm that day.

Sam Hoggard was aware of the size and value of the transaction as he had provided the cash.

Freda and Helen had planned the pickup procedure in detail, and the onward transportation to their holding premises in the CBD.

The night for the pickup seemed like any other to the casual passer-by. There was a slightly foggy, partial light glowing from commercial security at the Altona refinery, and mild but intermittent road traffic. It was easy for a nondescript dark-coloured SUV to drift on past a couple of times to check on any activity at the premises. Nothing untoward or suspicious. Freda and Helen were high on excitement and a small amount of self-administered stimulants. There were no obvious parked vehicles or lighting pods in the vicinity, so it was reasonable to assume 'all was normal'. At 1.35am they confidently drove onto the premises, parked around the back as agreed, turned off their SUV engine and cautiously walked across the parking area to enter the single unlighted back door, again as had been agreed. The door opened easily and quietly, and they walked along the hallway to a dimly lit area where two men in dark clothes, wearing masks and beanies, greeted them politely. The payment of the fifty percent cash outstanding was made with obvious care but without flourishes, and the drugs were then presented in well-contained packaging. All done in silence. Nods to show all in agreement, and then the exit in reverse from the way they had entered. A cautious peep out of the door into the car park, which seemed clear as Freda and Helen stepped outside.

All hell then broke loose. Bright lights flooded the car park and premises. Sirens wailed and police vehicles with red and blue flashing lights appeared from nowhere and screeched to a halt. Like stunned rabbits, the two women with a trolley full of packages stopped in their tracks.

There was a lot of jumbled noise but over it all came the clear command, "Stop! This is the police; you are under arrest, lie down flat where we can see your hands!"

The two inspectors Linda and Ian were leading the arresting police posse. Without hesitation, Helen pulled out a hand gun and fired straight at Linda, knocking her to the ground. An immediate reaction followed, first from Ian and then with two other police officers firing back and hitting Helen, who went down in a heap. Urgent calls were sent for an ambulance, which was close by. Then both attention and urgency were given to securing the premises and arresting the other two inhabitants.

As soon as Ian was sure that everything was securely controlled and locked down, he muttered to another officer, "A great pity about Helen Murphy, an ex-police officer; a tragedy about one so talented, she really was her own worst enemy."

The outcome was immense. Linda Alexander had been hit in the shoulder, and was rushed to hospital for repair, but the hit was not life threatening. Helen Murphy had been seriously wounded and died in hospital. Freda Zellerman was arrested and went into deep shock.

In due course, teams of experts arrived from multiple divisions to examine everything in and around the premises. Linda was able to be quickly back at work and was active in tidying up details. Her highest priority was to interview Freda Zellerman, and all levels of police headquarters were on high alert. The media was demanding updates with the usual insistence, and they were even more persistent when there had been injuries or deaths.

Rumours were rife and releases such as, "A witness is helping police with their enquiries" did not satisfying the media, who had unofficial information about a death, a witness who survived, and a high-level police officer who had been shot.

Chief Ron Brunton called for a media release to answer their questions. He issued the usual bland outline and added that the raid on the Kororoit Creek Road premises had realised the biggest yield of illegal drugs so far for the year. The usual methamphetamines, cannabis, quantities of cocaine, and unusual testosterone cypionate, viaplex, and provoplex, scheduled drugs that required authorisation, as used in body building, had been found.

He added that police HQ was delighted, and indicated that more arrests were to follow. He hoped that would take the immediate heat off media questions. Huge amounts of cash had been recovered and it was anticipated that more was to follow.

Ron Brunton had already issued orders to arrest Sam Hoggard and to carry out search warrants at both his home and office. Instructions had been given to the senior partner at Randle and Randle, Lawyers, that full cooperation was expected. In particular, a request was made for cousin Matthew Merriweather to be available at Randle and Randle for interview. The senior partner was a little surprised about the use of the word cousin.

44
The Outcome

Ricky Russo had disappeared. His car and passport were missing and his personal affairs were apparently all in order. However, his absence did not seem to be causing any concern and no family members — or anyone else — were insisting on an investigation. The mystery in certain circles was whether he had committed suicide. There was no talk of any link to the events described in the media.

Freda Zellerman was incarcerated while her interrogation continued. Her cooperation was essential for the arrest of Sam Hoggard, as it was obvious that he reported to a higher criminal, but it was not yet clear the extent of any involvement with Matthew Merriweather. Having practised as a solicitor for many years, Hoggard had a range of regular clients, most of whom it was expected had no criminal activities. Hoggard had been responsible for the formation and registration of trusts and shell companies, many of which were used by and for criminal activities. Unwinding them all would be a challenge, and would take time and be costly. Some people would have cause for grave concern.

Reggie McGuiness was considered an innocent bystander and the Matheson family, in spite of their great wealth, were not associated in any way with crime. The connection was mainly through social memberships at clubs and football socialising.

Hoggard would no doubt be going to prison for a long spell. Zellerman was destined for jail too, but with the cooperation she was now willingly giving, the sentence would be shortened. Linda and Ian speculated about how her generous body art would be greeted in jail.

The Bike Show was held with fewer drugs floating around than some had anticipated, and Cliff and Bria — for a real 'first' — had their super electric pushbikes included. It was great news to celebrate. Linda sent them congratulations.

45

John S. Silverman

John Silverman; the master criminal. He kept associates to the minimum, and minimised all records.

An arrest warrant was issued by the police on the basis of his ownership of the Kororoit Creek Road premises in Altona, and a search warrant issued for the premises in Mason Street, Creswick. The plan was to take into custody the 'caretaker' of that property, Guy Rackham. Speed was to be the essence of those actions.

Quite some time had elapsed since the last time Ricky Russo had been in touch with John Silverman and, being the quietly careful and astute person he was, Silverman asked around about Ricky's current whereabouts and activities. No feedback being received at all was cause for Silverman to be very cautious. The order for a large and varied range of "products" had also sent up a red flag.

With great intuition and timing, Silverman spent a Sunday afternoon and evening in his office in Lygon Street eliminating all written records that could be in any way incriminating and destroying any electronic equipment that might hold valuable data. He sent warnings to his associates involved with the properties in Collingwood and Creswick, and to others, that the police might be going to call.

The most lucrative part of his organisation, which was money laundering and associated gambling, would and could be reignited with his associates when appropriate, but he was sad about having to relinquish the riches he had acquired, particularly in antiques and classic vehicles. Any business in guns and ammunition had always been uncomfortable for him as it mainly involved dealing with bikies and less stable customers. The premises in Creswick had been a good hiding spot but that now was bound to be raided.

He set a delayed-start incendiary bomb in the middle of the offices, and sent a note to Reggie McGuiness and his assistant John Grey with an apology for the mess. Without a backwards look, he drove his Mercedes Benz to the airport and boarded a flight to the UK. All just before the arrest warrants were issued by the police. He was a 'loner' with no true allegiance to any one person, town or country. The UK beckoned as self-preservation overrode everything else. He then started plotting in his own mind detailed plans to pay back the harm created by his old associate Ricky Russo.

46
Congratulations

As was usual, Chief Superintendent Ron Brunton convened a group celebration to close off the 'Milly-Mandy' case. Tea, coffee and cakes, and members of the media were invited, plus representatives from the AFP, and Sergeant Beth Jenkins was brought in from Woodend.

Brunton issued warm thanks and congratulations to everyone involved. The usual team terminology was emphasised and details of some locations and limited names and addresses were used. He said what a pleasure it was to celebrate a good result with attention on many parts of the success.

He went on, "It also gives me great pleasure to report that our star Detective Inspector Linda Alexander has announced her engagement to Hugh Moorcraft, and I am well informed she has applied for leave to visit her family in Perth to introduce her partner!"

That received a laugh, and he added, "Hugh is not a policeman."

The questions and answers were free-flowing, including more personal questions about what next for DI Alexander, until CS Brunton called the event to a close, knowing full well that there would be drinks later. He did add that approaches from the AFP for Linda would be fought off, just as any enquiries from NZ Police would be blocked!

The End